The Invitation

As Sarah hesitated on the threshold of the room, peering inside, Morgan let out an exasperated sigh. And a second later, a hand between Sarah's shoulder blades sent her stumbling into the room. Unprepared, she lost her balance and fell to the floor. The door slammed shut behind her, and there was the sound of a key turning in the lock.

Sarah had no idea where she was or what she was doing there. But she knew, with sickening certainty, that the door would not open when she tried to turn the knob.

She was a prisoner.

Also in the
Point Horror series:

Look out for:

Point Horror

The Invitation

Diane Hoh

Hippo Books
Scholastic Children's Books
London

Scholastic Children's Books,
Scholastic Publications Ltd,
7-9 Pratt Street, London NW1 0AE, UK

Scholastic Inc.,
730 Broadway, New York, NY 10003, USA

Scholastic Canada Ltd,
123 Newkirk Road, Richmond Hill,
Ontario, Canada L4C 3G5

Ashton Scholastic Pty Ltd,
P O Box 579, Gosford, New South Wales,
Australia

Ashton Scholastic Ltd,
Private Bag 1, Penrose, Auckland,
New Zealand

First published in the US by Scholastic Inc., 1991
First published in the UK by Scholastic Publications Ltd, 1992

Copyright © Diane Hoh, 1991

ISBN 0 590 55060 8

Printed by Cox & Wyman Ltd, Reading, Berks

Chapter 1

The invitations were ready.

Twin towers of stiff, cream-colored envelopes stood sentry on the heavy antique desk in the sitting room next to Cassandra Rockham's powder-blue bedroom. The guest list, a single sheet of lined yellow paper, lay beside the ivory towers. A vivid red checkmark stabbed each name.

Cass leaned back lazily in the brown leather chair and stretched her legs, in buttery-soft suede jeans, lifting them until her booted feet rested on the shiny surface of the desk. Her thick, glossy black hair curved around her ears, brushing against her soft, pale cheeks. Her dark lashes flickered as she regarded the finished list with satisfaction.

One of her father's secretaries would seal, stamp, and mail the messages. In a day or two, selected mailboxes throughout the town of Greenhaven would announce Cass Rockham's annual Fall Party.

The best party.

The biggest.

The most important.

The lucky invited guests would be smiling, relieved to learn that they were still "in."

The unlucky ones . . . Cass shrugged carelessly. Who knew what the unlucky ones did when their mailboxes yielded only a handful of bills and a circular or two from discount stores?

It wasn't her fault some people just didn't belong at her parties.

Cass narrowed her chestnut-colored eyes in amusement as she pictured disappointed faces peering into mailboxes.

That's what people got for thinking she would add them to her list. Didn't she always invite the same people?

She grinned wickedly. Well . . . *almost* always.

It was weird, though, how there were always a few losers at school who would pass her in the hall after the invitations had been delivered and give her that dumb, nervous little look of hope, as if they thought she might not have known their address and intended to hand-deliver their "invite." They would actually slow their steps to give her the time to give it to them.

Sometimes, when she was in exactly the right kind of mood, she slowed her steps, too, relishing the way that tiny budding hope in their eyes sprang into full bloom.

Then Cass would smile broadly and hurry away, feeling completely guiltless. She couldn't help it if people were gullible sometimes.

Now that the invitations were ready to spread

their joy throughout Greenhaven, her party plans were all set.

The band, the best in five counties, had been signed for months. The caterer specialized in teen parties and knew better than to show up with trays of quiche or pâté or watercress sandwiches. The household staff had been busy for weeks, polishing and vacuuming every inch of the three-story white mansion. The heated pool sparkled, the acres of fall flowers and velvety lawns were immaculate, and the new Swedish sauna, a cedar hideaway in the woods near the stables, was finally fully operational.

The black strapless stretch dress, which her father had teasingly told Cass looked like a large belt, hung in its plastic bag in one of her closets. Her parents were packing for their thirty-day excursion to the south of France. They weren't the kind of parents who believed in chaperoning teen get-togethers. They were cool. They'd be gone before the party.

Everything was set. Everything was falling into place, as it always did for her parties.

Cass reached out a smooth white hand and tapped one of the creamy towers with a scarlet fingernail. A sly smile played at matching scarlet lips.

But this party would be a little bit different from the others. Besides dancing and eating and swimming, playing video games and maybe using the new sauna, there would be something new and interesting this year to *entertain* her guests.

Smiling to herself, Cass stood up, adjusted the

rolled-up sleeves of her peach silk blouse, and with one last satisfied glance at the twin towers on her desk, left the room.

As the heavy wooden door slammed shut behind her, the towers teetered for a moment, then toppled over. The crisp ivory envelopes tumbled forward, landing one at a time on the smooth, slippery surface of the desk. A few skated to the edge and over it, floating without a sound to the thick vanilla carpet below.

One card fell a couple of inches beyond the others, settling itself against the chair's leg.

The name and address on it were clearly visible.

In elegant script written with gold ink, the following guest was about to be invited to Cassandra Rockham's Fall Party:

Miss Sarah E. Drew
278 Valley Cove Drive
Greenhaven, New York

Chapter 2

On a hot autumn afternoon two days later, Sarah
Drew stood on the tiny front porch of her family's
squat yellow house surrounded by a neat but
unhealthy-looking lawn. She stared, open-mouthed
in shock, at the crisp ivory card lying unfolded in
the palm of her hand. She was a thin, pretty girl,
in khaki shorts and a white T-shirt, with hair the
color of beach sand pulled into a thick French braid
on her neck. Sarah frowned as she scanned the fine
gold engraving for the third time.

It had to be a mistake. Cass Rockham held a big,
semiformal party every October. That gave "Her
Royal Richness" time enough to cross off her invitation list any old friends who might have picked
up bad habits over the summer. It also gave her
time to cultivate any new and "suitable" arrivals at
Greenhaven High School.

The only new arrival this year, as far as Sarah
knew, was Shane Magruder. And Shane wasn't rich

enough, popular enough, or important enough to make Cass's guest list.

But then, Sarah told herself, neither am *I*. So what is this invitation doing in my mailbox?

Balancing the packet of mail in one hand, Sarah opened the front door with the other. All those parties Cass had held at the mansion up on the hill, and never once had Sarah Elizabeth Drew been invited. Never once had she expected to be. Never once had she *wanted* to be on that guest list. As far as Sarah was concerned, Cass Rockham and her entire "hill crowd" were completely unnecessary to the planet. Who needed them?

Not Sarah Drew.

So what was this invitation with the fancy gold printing doing in her hand?

The telephone in the kitchen shrilled. Probably her mother, calling from work to give instructions for dinner.

Dropping her backpack and the handful of bills and circulars on the worn tweed sofa, Sarah hurried into the small white kitchen.

She had barely said hello when Eleanor Whittier's voice began shrieking in her ear.

"Sarah! Sarah, is that you? Sarah, you'll never believe this, not in a zillion years! I've been invited to Cass's party! Can you believe it? Sarah, did you hear me?" All this spilled out of Eleanor without a single breath.

Sarah, her sandy brows furrowing, pictured Ellie in her pale yellow bedroom. Ellie's tall, broad body had to be quivering with excitement. It didn't take much to excite Ellie. Her blue eyes in her round, cheerful face were probably as shiny as the ocean on a sunny day, her cheeks pink as a sunset. She was probably clutching the invitation with an iron grip, afraid that it might suddenly leap out of her hand and scamper for the door.

Ellie didn't receive that many invitations. Only Sarah, Donald, Maggie, and now Shane had gotten to know the kind-hearted person behind the plain, honest face. How many times had Ellie gone out of her way to drive one of them home in lousy weather, loaned them notes from a class they'd missed, comforted a broken (or at least dented) heart? Too many times to count.

Ellie was a good friend to have. But her name didn't show up on that many guest lists. No wonder she was excited.

Ellie's voice gushed on, a waterfall of happiness. "I can't believe it! I mean, Cass smiled at me in the hall the other day, but I never thought — "

"Ellie, calm down," Sarah interrupted. "I got an invitation, too, which I, personally, think is extremely weird. There's something funny going on here, if you ask me."

The voice in Sarah's ear became even more excited. "You got one, too? That's great! That's fantastic! Oh, jeez, Sarah, what am I going to wear? I don't have anything pretty. What are you wearing?"

Sarah's straight, sparsely freckled nose wrinkled

in distaste. "Me? Are you kidding? You know how I feel about that crowd. I said I was invited, Ellie. I never said I was *going*."

Sarah heard nothing but a shocked silence at the other end of the telephone line.

Envisioning the horrified expression on Ellie's face, Sarah laughed. "Look," she said, sinking into a wooden chair at the round kitchen table, "it's probably a mistake. One of Mr. Rockham's secretaries must have goofed and invited the whole junior class by mistake. Cass will probably have her fired. Maybe killed."

"A mistake? Oh, no!"

"In the second place," Sarah said into the disappointed silence, "I have something important planned for that night." She glanced down at the invitation, still in her hand. "A week from Saturday, I'm cleaning Rover's bird cage."

"That's not funny!" Ellie scolded. Her voice held both disappointment and irritation.

Sarah felt as if she'd kicked a puppy. When was the last time Eleanor Whittier had had any reason to be this excited? It was her sister, Ruth, a thin, pretty senior who led the active social life Ellie yearned for.

"I'm sorry, Ellie," Sarah apologized. "But I have to be honest about this. If this is a mistake, it'll just hurt you more to get all freaked out about it and then be crushed."

"You don't know it's a mistake!" The words held a plea, begging Sarah to be wrong. "Cass *could* have invited us."

"Oh, sure," Sarah snapped, annoyed by Ellie's naked need to attend Cass's stupid party, "and there's going to be a flood in the Mojave Desert tomorrow at noon." Weren't they all okay without the friendship of Cass Rockham? Didn't she and Ellie, Maggie, Donald, and Shane have fun on their own? So they weren't a part of the hill crowd. So what? They had fun, didn't they?

"I'm going to call Donald," Ellie said stubbornly, "and see if he got an invitation, too."

Sarah's front doorbell rang. "You do that. Somebody's at the door. I'll call you back. 'Bye."

Shaking her head as she replaced the telephone, Sarah got up and hurried through the dim, cool house. She passed her violin, lying in its case on the dining room table. Her guilty conscience imagined the instrument crying out to her, "Hey, Sarah, what's the big idea? It's almost three-thirty!"

Every weekday for the past eight years, Sarah had practiced violin from three-fifteen until six-fifteen except on the days when she had orchestra practice after school. She knew that even if her mother hadn't insisted on the three-hour workout, she'd have done it, anyway. It relaxed her, calmed her down, taking her out of the real world, which wasn't always such a terrific place to be, and moving her into a world of peace and beauty. She would be lost without music, totally lost.

And it's not as if you have such a crowded social schedule that you have trouble finding time to practice, she told herself as she yanked open the front door.

Maggie Delaney and Shane Magruder stood in front of Sarah on the tiny front porch. They were a study in contrasts: Maggie tall and willowy, with copper-colored, short curly hair and freckled skin, dressed carelessly in blue sweatpants and a white sleeveless T-shirt; Shane tiny and fine-boned, her white-blonde hair hanging thick and straight to her shoulders, curved bangs reaching almost to her pale blue eyes. She was neatly dressed in a navy-blue cotton skirt and a matching short-sleeved flowered blouse.

Maggie was in soiled, scuffed sneakers; Shane in navy-blue flats. Sarah's best friends looked as mismatched as pizza and chocolate cake. But Maggie had taken shy, quiet Shane under her wing immediately after Shane's arrival in town last June and their personalities had quickly meshed.

Maggie's enthusiasm for "the new girl" had made it easier for the others to accept Shane into their little group. Sarah wasn't sorry. Shane was quiet and it was hard to know what she was thinking, but she didn't have a mean bone in her body and she loved music.

Sarah knew instantly why they were on her front porch. Maggie's thickly lashed brown eyes were gleaming with excitement. In one hand, which she thrust triumphantly toward Sarah, lay another of the cream-colored rectangles.

Sarah groaned. She checked Shane's hands. The left one held an identical card, gingerly, with only the fingertips, as if Shane were afraid it would bite her. Sarah couldn't tell if the thought of attending Cass's party frightened Shane, or if she was simply confused about receiving an invitation.

"So . . . you got one, too," Sarah said flatly, opening the door wider to let them in. "This is really too weird. Any idea what's going on?"

Maggie pushed past her into the house, yanking Shane in along with her. "We've been invited, that's what's going on. Finally! It's about time Cass Rockham noticed us! She must have realized that no party would be complete without our stimulating presence." She plopped down on the sofa in the living room. The late-afternoon sun streaming in through the window painted her copper hair with golden highlights. "I mean, we may not be big deals on campus, Sarah, but we're not exactly nerds either." She grinned. "I, for instance, am a drum majorette with the marching band. That is not something to be taken lightly."

Sarah grinned back. "*Dumb* majorette, did you say?"

Maggie threw a pillow at her.

The phone rang again.

"I'll bet that's Donald," Maggie said cheerfully, following Sarah into the kitchen. "He probably just got around to checking his mail. Bet you a dollar he got an invite, too. Probably because he made Varsity basketball this year. Cass has a thing for athletes. Maybe that's why we all got invited. Because we know Donald."

She was right about it being Donald on the phone.

Donald Neeson had been invited to Cass's party. He seemed very anxious to find out if Maggie, too, had been invited.

That puzzled Sarah. Donald already had a girlfriend, someone named Dolly. He'd met her during the summer. They were both counsellors at a summer camp not far from town. Because she lived in a distant town, none of them had met her yet, but Donald had talked about her a lot. So why was he so eager to find out if Maggie was going to Cass's party?

"Yeah, Maggie's been invited," Sarah told him. "And I think she's probably going. She's jumping out of her skin over here. You'd think she'd been invited to the White House."

"Cass's house *is* white," Maggie whispered devilishly in Sarah's ear.

"Ellie's probably going, too," Sarah added, ignoring Maggie, "if these invitations aren't a mistake, which they probably are. And Shane will go if Maggie goes. Me, I wouldn't be caught dead at one of Cass's parties. I don't know why we got these invitations, but I've got better things to do with my time than hang around with that crowd. I can't believe you guys are all so hyper about this. We never went before, and we didn't miss it, did we? *Did* we?"

"Well, no," Donald admitted. "But if Maggie's going . . ."

This is a new wrinkle, Sarah thought, frowning. Except for Shane, they'd all been friends for ages and Donald had never seemed romantically interested in Maggie. He'd dated lots of girls, but never Maggie.

And what about the absent Dolly? It certainly didn't sound like he was planning to take an out-of-town guest to the party. How would Dolly take the idea of Donald going to a big bash without her?

She'd better be awfully understanding.

"Come on over," Sarah told him with a sigh, deciding that this party business probably wasn't going to just disappear as she wanted it to. Maggie was hovering near her elbow, Shane was waiting on the couch, and Ellie was waiting to hear from Sarah again. Might as well get it settled right now, one way or the other.

She'd have trouble concentrating on her music, anyway, until they'd decided what to do about the invitations.

"Stop and pick up Ellie on your way," she told Donald before hanging up. "We'll talk about the party here."

As she put the telephone back in its cradle, Sarah told herself with firm resolve that no one was going to talk her into attending one of Cass Rockham's idiotic parties.

No one!

Chapter 3

"I'm *not* going," Sarah said firmly when her living room was full of her four closest friends. "I can't stand Cass Rockham or any of her pals, and that house of hers scares me. It sits up there on top of the hill like some ugly white giant looking down on its cowering subjects. Us. The entire town. I hate that place."

No one laughed. The Rockham mansion, the only building occupying the hill, intimidated all of them. There was no other house in town like it. But then, no one else in town had the Rockham fortune. No one even came close.

It was Maggie who zeroed in first on Sarah's resolve. "You don't hate *all* of Cass's friends. A certain person with dark brown hair and brown eyes and a build to die for is a good friend of Cass's. He'll be at the party, Sarah."

Sarah felt heat searing her cheeks. Maggie meant Riley. Riley White.

I never should have told her that I thought he was cute, she thought irritably. But that was before

I knew he was tight with Rockham's crowd. Of course . . . I know it now, and I still think he's cute.

Cass's friend or not, Riley White had the greatest smile Sarah had ever noticed on a boy. He often waited for friends in front of his locker outside her English class during the last few minutes before the bell rang. Sarah sat in the first row and could see him through the door window.

He was tall, but not skinny like Donald, with thick dark, straight hair. His clothes — thick sweaters or crisp dress shirts with the sleeves rolled up — looked expensive, but the smile that he flashed when someone walked by assured her that he wasn't a snob.

She knew he was a football player, and that he drove a canary-yellow sports car, but that was all she knew about him. Except that he couldn't possibly be in the market for a girlfriend. Not him. He probably had several. Dozens, maybe.

And even if, by some miracle, he wasn't dating anyone, he certainly wouldn't be interested in a violinist who lived in a little yellow house on Valley Cove Drive and wasn't part of the "in" crowd.

Well, she'd lived without Riley White in her life for seventeen years, and she'd done okay so far. She didn't need him.

But that smile . . .

"Come on, Sarah!" Maggie persisted. "You'll be the prettiest girl at the party. How could Riley not notice you?" She grinned. "Besides, aren't you dying to see how the filthy rich live? I hear they've got stables up there and a heated pool and a sauna.

. . . C'mon, Sarah, it'll be a blast! Please? For the rest of us? We couldn't go without *you!*"

Then Donald and Ellie put more pressure on Sarah. Ellie, thrilled by her invitation, couldn't believe Sarah's hesitation, while Donald was clearly afraid that if Sarah refused to go, Maggie might, too.

"My mother will have a fit," Sarah protested when all of her other excuses had been brushed away. "She thinks parties are an incredible waste of time. And you guys are keeping me from practicing just by arguing about this. Why don't you all go home so I can get to work?"

"Sarah," Maggie said firmly, "all you ever do is practice and study. Your mom can't possibly complain about one teeny, weeny little party!"

Sarah couldn't help laughing. "Maggie, calling Cass Rockham's Fall Party 'little' is like calling Buckingham Palace a 'cute little cottage.' "

It was Shane who finally decided Sarah. "I think you should make up your own mind," she said quietly when the other three had tired of arguing. Her lovely face was completely serious. "Don't ever, ever let anyone talk you into doing something you don't want to do." Then she added in a normal voice, "I'll go if the rest of you do. My mom's been after me to make more of an effort socially. She says I've been staying at home too much since we moved here."

Sarah, watching Shane, wondered, not for the first time, what that look in her pale blue eyes meant. Was it sadness? Did Shane miss her old friends, her old home? Was that it? Spending your junior year in a new town, a new school, could be awful, Sarah was sure of that. But wasn't what she saw more than simple sadness? Sometimes Shane's eyes looked almost . . . haunted.

Making up her mind, Sarah announced reluctantly, "Okay, I'll go. I don't want to spoil anyone's fun. And I guess it *could* be all right. But I'm warning you, if it's a bust, I'm leaving early, whether any of the rest of you do or not."

A chorus of cheers filled the small living room.

Maggie grinned. "It was my argument about Riley that did it," she boasted. "Sometimes I'm so clever, I scare myself."

Donald moved closer to Maggie on the couch, a shy smile on his bony face. Ellie, sitting awkwardly on a straight-backed wooden chair against the wall, wanted to know what Sarah was going to wear to the party.

But the question that kept Sarah from rejoicing with her best friends was why Cassandra Rockham, who probably couldn't even match their names to their faces, had suddenly decided to invite the five of them to her Fall Party.

Something about this whole thing just didn't feel right to Sarah.

Chapter 4

When Eleanor Whittier told her sister, Ruth, about the invitation to Cass Rockham's party, Ruth shrieked.

"You? She invited *you*?" As thin and pretty as Ellie was square and plain, Ruth possessed a sharp, unpredictable temper that made people who knew her uneasy. "She couldn't have invited you! It's got to be a mistake." Ruth's dark, wiry hair stood out like an electrified bush around her angular face. Her small, dark eyes blazed with fury. "She must have gotten our names mixed up!"

Reaching out long, pointy, fuchsia fingernails, Ruth demanded, "Let me see that invitation, Ellie."

Ruth had once locked her baby sister in the cellar for hours. On another occasion, she had buried Ellie's favorite doll in the backyard and refused to reveal its location until forced to by their mother. Ruth was not a good person to defy.

Her round, sky-blue eyes fearful, Ellie obediently handed over the precious rectangle and the envelope that had held it. Her name was printed clearly on the front.

Ruth could find no evidence of a mistake. The envelope had obviously been intended for *Eleanor* Whittier.

"I don't believe this," Ruth said, shaking her head. "You don't even *know* her!"

A sudden flash of bravery led Ellie to snatch back her invitation. "Neither do you," she said, turning to leave her sister's room.

"I do, too! She's in my gym class."

The knowledge that for once in her life she had something her big sister wanted made Ellie defiant. "I'll bet she doesn't even know your name."

Ruth's face twisted with rage. "You stupid cow, get out of my room! That invitation is a mistake. Cass would never invite a loser like you to one of her parties." Her breath came in ragged gasps. Her face flushed an ugly purple. She began shoving at Ellie, pushing her forcibly toward the door. "You'll see! You'll get there and no one will pay any attention to you except to make fun of the way you look. Then you'll know what a fool you are." Her voice rose. "Now, get *out*! Get out of my room!" And she shoved Ellie, hard.

Ellie stumbled, regained her balance, and found herself in the hallway, her body shaking in response to Ruth's terrible wrath.

But the invitation was still grasped firmly in her own hand. It was hers! And mistake or not, she was going to Cass Rockham's party.

Now all she had to do was find a dress that would

look good on her, a dress that would make her look like she belonged at the Rockham mansion, no matter what Ruth said. Finding a dress like that wouldn't be easy. All the really pretty dresses were made for small girls like Shane, or tall, thin girls like Maggie and Sarah.

Trying to forget her sister's wild fury, Eleanor Whittier went shopping.

Shane's mother was as excited about the party as Shane had anticipated. "That big house up on the hill?" she cried, cradling the invitation in her hands. "Oh, honey, that's wonderful! What a perfect opportunity to make new friends."

Shane slid into a metal chair on the patio, where her mother was busy potting white and yellow flowers. Toying nervously with a lock of pale hair, Shane said quietly, "I'd rather stay home, but — " She was about to add, "But my friends are going, so I guess I will, too," when her horrified mother interrupted her.

"Stay home? Shane, are you crazy? This is your chance to make a great new start, to make the right kind of friends — "

It was Shane's turn to interrupt. "I *have* the right kind of friends, Mother," she said coolly.

But she knew how her mother felt about Donald and Maggie, Ellie and Sarah. According to Mrs. Magruder, Maggie was "a bundle of nerves," Ellie was "rather ordinary-looking," Donald "too shy," and although Shane's mother admired Sarah's brilliant mind, she had pointed out gently that Sarah spent far too much time practicing and studying to ever be really popular.

It astonished Shane that, after everything that had happened back in Rockport, her mother still expected life to be normal here in Greenhaven. Couldn't she see that all Shane wanted to do was crawl into bed and hide there forever? Moving to another town, a new house, a new school, hadn't changed anything. Only those four friends her mother disapproved of had kept her from shutting herself off from the world.

It had been Maggie at first who, with her bubbly friendliness, had pulled Shane back into the real world. Then Donald, with his shy smile and husky voice, then Ellie with her warm sense of humor and, finally, Sarah, so smart and so down-to-earth. Slowly they had drawn a very shaken Shane into their little group. She had thought she would never trust anyone again, but the four had proved her wrong.

She didn't want any more new friends. She liked the ones she had.

"You have to put the past completely behind you," her mother said. "What happened back in Rockport is over and done with, sweetie. You made a mistake. We all make them. No one here knows what happened. So you can be a part of any group you want." She waved the invitation in Shane's face. "And this looks like your ticket into a very *good* group."

Shane stood up abruptly. "I've already met the best group in town, Mother." She began moving toward the doorway. There, she turned and added, "Don't worry. I'll go to the party. But the friends I'm going with are the only friends I need."

Then she went down the hall and into her bedroom, where she lay down on top of the thick quilt, shivering with a sudden chill. If her new friends knew the truth about her, would they still like her?

Or would they turn on her the way everyone in Rockport had?

Shane was suddenly very tired. Hoping that she wouldn't be awakened, screaming, by the same nightmare again, Shane closed her eyes and shut out everything but the sound of her own breathing until sleep overtook her.

Several blocks away, in his own bedroom, Donald Neeson wrestled with his conscience. Did he really need to tell Dolly about Cass's party? That could be risky. He knew exactly how the phone conversation would go. She'd say, "Oh, great, Donald! A party! What fun! What should I wear?"

And then he'd have to say he wasn't supposed to bring a guest, and she'd throw a fit at the thought of him going without her. She might even suspect that it wasn't true, that he could bring someone if he really wanted to. Which he could. That place of Cass's was so huge, she'd never even know Dolly was there.

He *could* take her if he wanted to. But the truth was, he *didn't* want to. Taking Dolly with him would spoil any chance he had of letting Maggie know how he felt — something he hadn't even been sure of himself until a couple of weeks ago. He'd been gone all summer working as a counsellor at a camp for kids, and although he'd missed all of his friends, it had been Maggie's face he'd seen every night before he fell asleep.

That had surprised him. Maggie? His pal, Maggie? Since when had he started thinking about her *that* way — not like a pal, but like a girl he wanted to date? The idea had really knocked him out.

But then he'd met Dolly, another counsellor. She was pretty and a leader at camp. Tall and blonde, she'd seemed more sophisticated, more remote, than the other girls. He'd been flattered that she'd been interested in him instead of one of the older guys. And she'd helped him forget how much he missed Maggie.

Now, even though she lived half an hour away in a suburb called Willowcreek, she still thought of them as a couple, a twosome, a pair. But the truth was, Donald had hardly missed her at all since he'd returned home. It was as if he'd automatically left her behind along with the little kids, the lake, and the nightly camp fires.

And after the first time he'd seen Maggie again, glowing with a summer tan, her braces finally off, her coppery hair streaked with gold ribbons by the sun, the evenings spent around the camp fire with Dolly slid further back into a tiny little corner of his mind and stayed there.

And he *had* tried, more than once, to ease away from Dolly. But each time, she had become so upset that he'd chickened out and let the matter drop.

He'd been glad each time that he hadn't mentioned Maggie's name. Dolly had been so angry . . . there was no telling what she might do.

"Dork!" he accused his mirror image with contempt. "You know it's Maggie you want to be with at that party. But Dolly still thinks it's her. Be a man and tell her the truth! And make her understand that you mean it this time."

He would. He would do that.

He'd tell her Saturday night. Dolly had invited him for dinner at the apartment she shared with a friend. Because she had no family, she worked as a waitress full time during the day and took classes toward her high school equivalency diploma at night. He'd been impressed by that. It meant Dolly had goals and didn't give up on them.

Now, he had to face the fact that it also meant she didn't give up on anything (or anybody) she wanted. And she seemed to want Donald Neeson.

But he would end it. And if Dolly didn't understand, well that was her problem, not his. Wasn't it?

Maggie Delaney literally danced home from Sarah's house. A party! A great party! At the Rockham place. What a hoot!

She had never thought Sarah would agree to go. Parties just weren't Sarah's thing. Study, practice, study, practice, that was Sarah's life. It was amazing that she had a sense of humor at all, but she did. And it was time she lightened up a little. A sense of humor probably needed a good party once in a while, the way muscles needed exercise. As her friend, Maggie thought, it was my duty to talk her into that party. I'm glad I did it.

It was also way past time for a little romance in Sarah's life. Riley White would be at the party. Sarah would look absolutely beautiful, and Riley would ask her to dance. . . .

Donald Neeson would be there, too. Maggie's long legs did a little jig on the sidewalk and her lips curved into an impish grin. Everyone else saw Donald as a quiet, shy "brainy" sort of guy who just happened to play a great game of basketball. Everyone but her. She was convinced there was more to Donald than what people saw.

And she intended to find out if she was right. Cass's party would be the perfect time and place to do that.

Maggie's grin disappeared suddenly. If only Donald didn't bring that . . . that person he'd met at camp. What was her name? Dolly? What a dumb name! She was probably big and blonde and an eyelash-batter. She couldn't possibly be right for Donald.

It didn't bother her that Donald had had a summer romance. Lots of people did that at camp. No big deal. Besides, she hadn't known how she felt about Donald when he left for camp.

But it was fall now. Time for Donald to forget about camp and what's-her-name and get on with things.

Things like developing what Maggie was sure they were *both* feeling. She could tell Donald felt something, too, by the way he acted around her, the looks he gave her.

But Donald was shy. That was one of the things she liked about him. I, she thought with a grin, am *not*. So I'll just have to help things along.

The bounce in her step returned as she hurried home.

Sarah shared none of her friends' enthusiasm for the upcoming party. Lovingly taking her violin from its case and positioning it in its familiar niche near her collarbone, she thought grimly, If only I could back out, tell them I've changed my mind.

But she had promised her friends. And Sarah wasn't one to break her promises.

She couldn't stop wondering why she and her friends had been invited to Cass's party. But right now something else stuck in her mind — something about her friends' reactions. Something had seemed out of place, but she couldn't quite put her finger on it.

Opening the sheet music on the metal stand in front of her, Sarah placed the instrument under her chin and lifted her bow.

Before she began, she paused, suddenly realizing what was bothering her.

Why hadn't Shane, a new girl who should welcome the opportunity to attend such a large, important party, been more enthusiastic about her invitation? Why had Shane reacted so strangely?

Chapter 5

Ellie couldn't believe her good luck. The dress was perfect. A blaze of royal blue and emerald green panels on a slender column of silky fabric, the dress lay spread out on her bed like a peacock's tail. Dressed only in her slip, her brown hair in beige rollers, Ellie smiled down at the miracle dress, the dress that slimmed her, put a light in her blue eyes and made her feel like the pretty person she had always wanted to be.

Ruth, sitting on Ellie's extra bed painting her toenails, was not smiling. Still burning from the humiliation of finding out that her sister's invitation was not mistakenly meant for her, Ruth glowered at the splash of silky color atop Ellie's quilt.

"You're *not* going to have a good time, Ellie," she said, studying the wads of cotton separating her toes. "No one's going to pay any attention to you. You don't belong at that party, and you know it."

But Ellie, riding high on the wonder of the way she looked in the dress, shook her head. "I *am* going to have a good time, Ruthie. I'm going to have the best night of my life. I'll tell you all about it to-morrow."

Ruth's dark eyes flashed with anger. She jabbed at a toe with bright purple polish, her mouth twisted nastily. "You think I want to hear about your miserable evening? Guess again! You can go cry on someone else's shoulder when you realize how stupid you've been!"

Ignoring that, Ellie danced into the bathroom to remove the rollers from her hair and put on her makeup.

When she returned, Ruth was gone.

Breathing a sigh of relief, Ellie bent to pick up her dress.

And screamed in horror.

There, settled on the bodice, smack in the center where it couldn't be missed, like some repulsive, fat insect, was a huge, bright purple blob of nail polish.

Shouting for her mother, Ellie grabbed the dress and ran to the bathroom, where she began scrubbing frantically at the ugly blotch.

By the time her mother came rushing in to see what was wrong, a sobbing Ellie was sitting on the edge of the tub, the purple-streaked dress in her hands a total ruin.

"Oh, Ellie, what happened?" Mrs. Whittier cried. "Heavens, you weren't doing your nails in that dress, were you?"

Ellie lifted her tearstained face. "No. It was Ruth. She did it."

"Well, it must have been an accident," her

mother said matter-of-factly. "Now, let's just see what we can do to repair the damage." She gently tugged the dress out of Ellie's lifeless hands.

But it was hopeless. The polish clung to the dress, hardening into stubborn rivulets.

Ruth is evil, Ellie thought dully, watching her mother's futile efforts. She didn't want me to go to this party, and now she's made sure that I can't. I don't have anything else to wear.

"You sit right here," her mother said, patting Ellie's shoulder. "I'll be back in a second."

When she returned, she was carrying a pale green dress with long sleeves, a row of gaudy, bright gold buttons marching down the front, a wide gold belt circling the waist. "We're the same size," she said cheerfully. "I'll bet anything this will fit you. Try it on, honey."

It fit.

But the difference between the way she looked in the simple blue and green sheath and the way she looked in the matronly, sickly-pastel shirtwaist dress with its garish buttons and belt brought fresh tears to Ellie's eyes.

I look, she thought dismally, like a fat clump of celery.

This was all Ruth's fault. How could she have been so cruel?

"Oh, honey, come on," her mother said gently. "It's not that bad. You look pretty. Really, you do." She sighed. "It's either this or staying home. You don't want to do that, do you?"

No, Ellie didn't want to do that. This party was

too important. Besides, she couldn't give Ruth that satisfaction.

As she descended the stairs, wearing the pale green dress, her makeup repaired, her eyes only slightly reddened and puffy, Ruth's thin face appeared in the doorway of her bedroom.

"You've got no business going," she said harshly. "You'll be sorry."

"Donald, I'm warning you," Dolly's voice, shrill with anger, threatened from the other end of Donald's telephone line, "if you go to this party without me, you'll regret it! I told you Saturday night, you can't get rid of me that easily."

Donald, already dressed for the party in crisp khaki slacks and a rust-colored sweater under a tan sportcoat, flinched. He'd been expecting her call. He'd told her the truth last Saturday night. It hadn't been easy. The minute he'd mentioned that they should both "see other people," Dolly had thrown a fit, revealing a side of her he'd never seen before.

He'd thought she was so sophisticated, so cool. It scared him that he could be so wrong about someone.

"You think you can dump me, just like that?" she'd shouted, her face contorted into something foreign. It had been hard for Donald to remember, at that moment, what he'd ever seen in Dolly. She frightened him, with her mouth all twisted and her eyes little angry slits.

"You can't just walk in here and tell me we're

finished," she'd hissed, waving a curled fist in his face. "Or that you're going to some big fancy bash with your friends and you're not inviting me along. I won't stand for that, Donald!"

He'd barely mentioned Maggie, being careful to make her a part of the group. Some instinct warned him that Dolly probably shouldn't know he had another girl on his mind. That wouldn't be safe for Maggie.

But Dolly was suspicious, anyway, and hammered at him with questions about there being another girl. He denied it, for Maggie's sake; still, he was pretty sure Dolly didn't believe him.

Donald hadn't backed down. He had, in fact, insisted that their relationship was over and that he was going to the party. But he'd known when he left Dolly's apartment that it *wasn't* over. He knew he hadn't seen or heard the last of his summer romance.

And now, just as he'd feared, here she was on the phone, threatening him.

"Donald? Are you still there?"

"Look, Dolly," he said carefully, anxious to get going, "I have to hang up now. I'll talk to you tomorrow, okay?" And he would, he resolved firmly. He'd drive over to Willowcreek tomorrow and make it clear, once and for all, that it was *over*. "You wouldn't have had a good time at the party, anyway," he added in an effort to calm her anger. "You wouldn't know anyone there but me. That wouldn't be much fun for you."

After a moment of uneasy silence, Dolly's voice said softly, "You won't have a good time, either, Donald. Not without me. I promise you that."

"You look absolutely beautiful," Shane's mother gushed, her hands clasped together in front of her as if she were giving thanks. "I'm so glad you accepted this invitation. It proves to your father and me that you're serious about making a fresh start here. And that's all we want. My, that dress is so pretty!"

Shane agreed. It was. Her mother had insisted on buying her a new dress, even though she already owned several party dresses. She'd worn them to parties in Rockport. Her mother didn't want her wearing one of those. She was superstitious and thought it would be "begging for bad luck."

The new dress was bright red . . . blood-red, Shane thought gloomily, with tiny sleeves and a short, full skirt. It was a very . . . happy dress.

So why did she feel just the opposite? Why did she have such a bad feeling about the night ahead?

"You'll have a wonderful time," Mrs. Magruder said as Shane slipped into a pair of black heels and picked up her black clutch bag.

I don't think so, Shane thought with conviction. And wondered, as she often did, what her old friends in Rockport were doing tonight.

Was there a party in Rockport tonight?

And if there was, would her old friends miss her?

I don't think so, she thought again. I don't think they'll miss me at all.

Aloud, she said simply, "I'll try to have fun, Mom. I will."

But she knew as she left the house that she didn't mean it.

"Maggie, stand still!" Sarah ordered. "I can't fasten this necklace when you're jumping up and down like a yo-yo."

Maggie grinned and forced herself to stand still, arms held stiffly at her sides. The black dress with spaghetti straps and sarong skirt was from last year's spring dance, but Donald hadn't been there, so he hadn't seen it yet. And she knew it looked great on her tall, wiry body. She had twisted her copper curls into a bun at the back of her head, leaving a few rusty tendrils tickling her ears. The silver necklace, a tiny seagull on a delicate chain, was the finishing touch.

"You look beautiful," Sarah said softly. "Donald will flip!" She envied Maggie's mood, but her friend's excitement wasn't contagious. This evening felt all wrong to Sarah. Uneasiness clung to her, wrapping her in its clammy grasp.

Her mother had had a fit over the invitation. "Don't be ridiculous," she had fumed. "You don't have time for such nonsense. You've got that recital in two weeks, and that English paper due. You need every spare moment you can find."

Until that moment, Sarah hadn't even wanted to go to the party. Only Maggie's persuasive powers had led her to consider the idea.

But, faced with her mother's disapproval, Sarah

had a strong urge not only to accept the invitation, but to try her darnedest to have a good time. She was suddenly very tired of doing nothing but practicing the violin and studying.

And Riley White's smiling face seemed to be floating in front of her eyes, encouraging her.

"I'm *going* to this party," she had told her mother firmly.

And then she'd gone straight to the mall and bought a dress.

It was beautiful. In an autumn color the saleslady called "Burnt Bronze" and Sarah called, simply, "gold," it set off the last of her tan and put golden highlights in her brown eyes. The soft folds of the calf-length skirt whispered against her legs as she walked, and the V-neck and short sleeves flattered her slenderness. Maggie had intertwined gold ribbon through Sarah's thick French braid and loaned her a pair of tiny golden hoops for her ears.

"You look pretty special yourself," Maggie responded to Sarah's compliment. "I just wish you'd quit acting like you were going to a funeral. What's *wrong* with you?"

Sarah wasn't sure. She only knew that the evening loomed ahead of her like a huge monster waiting in the dark to devour her.

Maybe it was because she felt guilty about going against her mother's wishes.

Or maybe it was because she still wondered why she and her friends had been invited to this party. At school, Cass and her crowd weren't paying any more attention to them than they ever had. Nothing had changed. The five of them still didn't exist as far as the hill crowd was concerned.

So why the invitations?

What was Cassandra Rockham up to?

"Party time!" Maggie cried, holding her bedroom door open for Sarah. "Donald's picking us up in two minutes. Let's go!"

Sarah sighed. It was too late to back out now.

Chapter 6

Sarah's heart sank as Donald's car approached the huge white Rockham mansion sprawled across the top of the hill. It was even more intimidating than she'd imagined.

The very size of the house, three broad stories of white towering above arriving visitors, was awesome. Tall, fat pillars stood guard at the wide porch, as if to say: No one unsuitable will be allowed entry.

And far, far below lay the town. Too far away, Sarah thought dismally, for any hilltop screams to reach a resident's ears. And then she wondered what on earth had made her think such a thing.

Maybe it had something to do with how dark the house was. Where were all the lights? Shouldn't a party house filled with guests be ablaze with warm, welcoming brightness?

This one wasn't. There were only faint glimmers of pale yellow flickering faintly from most of the long, narrow windows, including those at the very top of the structure. It was as if the mansion were shrouded in fog.

But there was no fog.

"Maybe they forgot to pay their electric bill," Maggie quipped.

No one laughed.

"Wonder what's with the *Dark Shadows* look?" Donald said. "It's too early for a Halloween party."

Donald parked, and they all climbed out of the car. Although music and laughter filled the warm autumn night, Sarah felt a sudden, inexplicable stab of fear. The mansion *sounded* the way a party house should. But there was something . . . something wrong. She felt it. It touched her, like an icy finger, deep inside her bones.

Sarah watched Donald hurry to Maggie. Maggie and Donald had been friends for a long time. It seemed weird that they'd all of a sudden discovered each other. Remembering the look in Donald's eyes when he saw Maggie in the black dress, Sarah wondered if anyone would ever look at her like that.

Maggie, a look of happy expectancy dancing across her freckled face, rang the doorbell.

A smiling Cass, in a skintight tiny little black dress, answered the ring. Her welcome was enthusiastic, although Sarah noticed that Cass called none of them by name.

That's probably because, Sarah thought drily, she doesn't have the slightest idea what our names *are*. So why did she invite us? What kind of person invited strangers to a party?

Sarah wasn't sure she wanted to know the answer to that question.

"Must have given the servants the night off," she

murmured to Shane and Ellie, who hovered nervously behind her. Ellie kept tugging at the pale green dress, as if constantly rearranging it might improve it. Sarah had never seen Shane so pale. The bright-red dress, as pretty as it was, didn't help. It made Shane's pale hair and eyes and stark-white skin look almost lifeless.

Lifeless? Sarah shivered. What a horrible thought! What was the matter with her tonight?

Cass ushered them inside, chatting cheerfully about the decorations. She said nothing about the lack of light as she led them through a noisy, crowded, but dimly lit foyer the size of Sarah's entire house. The only light came from tall, thick, salmon-colored candles on gold metal stands stationed in the corners. Sarah could see from the shadows dancing across the long hallway stretching ahead of them, that the rooms were also lit only by candles.

"I hope they didn't skimp on smoke detectors in this place," she murmured to Ellie.

The shadows added to Sarah's anxiety. Was Cass aiming for a "romantic setting"? Or did she have something else in mind? Something that would justify the nervous gnawing in Sarah's stomach?

Cass led them immediately into a long narrow room panelled in rich, dark wood. It, too, was lighted only by groups of candles perched on a refreshment table at one end of the room and on bookshelves at the opposite end. The center of the room was deep in shadow.

But Sarah could see that a dozen or more guests

were seated silently on a double column of wooden straight-backed chairs placed back-to-back in the center of the room. Four of the chairs were unoccupied. Not *five*, as Sarah would have expected, but *four*. Which one of the newest arrivals was going to be without a chair?

It was an odd sight, and Sarah whispered to Shane, "Maybe we're going to play choo-choo train." Shane gave no sign that she'd heard. Her eyes were wide with doubt, and Sarah could see that she was already beginning to regret accepting her invitation. No wonder. This party, so far, looked *too* weird.

The guests' faces were lost in shadow. Sarah wondered if Riley White was seated on one of the chairs.

"Hey, look at that," Donald said as the group of five stood uncertainly in the doorway.

Sarah followed his gaze and found, high up on the wall at one end of the room, a small television set and, to its far left, a camera.

Were they being filmed?

"Their security system, I bet," Donald said knowingly. "They probably have that set-up in every room of the house. Maybe even out on the grounds."

That made sense. There would be plenty to steal in the mansion, Sarah thought. Cass's wardrobe alone would bring a small fortune.

But just then, Cass flipped a switch and the television screen was filled with a rock group. Sarah thought it was MTV until Cass said, "That's Evil

Deeds, the group that's playing in the ballroom. We can see it in here because that's a closed-circuit television up there. Neat, huh?"

But no sound came from the set.

Sarah spotted Riley White, wearing a V-neck sweater and leaning against a side wall talking to a pretty girl in a blue dress. One of his booted feet was resting on one of the chairs. Did that mean it was his and no one else could sit on it? Or was he just tired?

"You look better than her," Maggie whispered loyally, noticing the direction of Sarah's gaze.

Sarah smiled and began to say something. But she was interrupted by her hostess, who was standing in front of the refreshment table, clinking a fork against a glass.

"There isn't any sound up there," she said, pointing to the screen, "because we're going to make our own music. We're going to play musical chairs."

A wave of groans encircled the room.

Riley White looked Sarah's way just then, and he smiled. Candle shadows played across his face, softening its angles. Sarah suddenly felt that even had there been no light at all, she'd have seen that smile.

Unsure, she glanced over her shoulder. Maybe he was smiling at someone behind her.

There wasn't anyone behind her.

She smiled back.

Cass clapped her hands and called out, "Okay, everyone, you all know how to play, right?" Without waiting for an answer, she continued, "I'll turn the music on. Then you all start marching around the chairs. When I stop the music, everyone grab a chair. One person will be left without one. That," Cass said smugly, "will be the *loser*."

"Doesn't she make it sound as if the loser would be taken out and shot?" Sarah whispered to Ellie.

Ellie smiled uncertainly and quickly returned her attention to Cass.

Sarah was puzzled. Musical chairs wasn't the kind of entertainment she expected at a party held by the most sophisticated girl at Greenhaven High School. It was a kids' game. There must be more to this game than Cass was letting on, Sarah decided.

"Each time the music stops, a chair will be removed," Cass continued. "That way, you'll always be short one chair. I only have five consolation prizes, so when five people are out of the game, it ends. Any questions?"

At the phrase "five people," Sarah's scalp tingled. She had come tonight with four friends. There was no way Cass could know *which* five people would lose, was there?

"I thought we were going to dance," the girl standing next to Riley whined. "And it's too dark in here for a dumb kids' game. We'll be bumping into each other all over the place. Do we really have to do this?"

"Yes, we do," Cass insisted firmly, moving to a portable cassette player stationed on one end of the refreshment table. "It'll be fun! And you have to listen carefully, because I'm not giving you any warning before I stop the music. Take your places, please!"

Although there were more groans and some muttered grumbling, the guests lined up around the double row of chairs. Sarah glanced at Eleanor, standing beside her looking unhappy. Ellie, Sarah knew, hated this game. Heavy even as a child, she had never moved fast enough to grab an empty chair when the music stopped so abruptly. Ellie was always the first to lose.

And tonight was no exception. When the music stopped, Ellie was rounding a corner. Everyone else promptly slid into empty chairs, while Ellie stood at the end of the column looking unhappy, her mouth open in dismay.

Sarah felt sorry for her. It was a dumb game. Someone always got left out. She watched Ellie struggle to play the "good sport." Her face held the same look of misery she wore in gym when no one picked her for a team, but she fought to force a fake smile onto her face and finally succeeded.

"Too bad, you lose!" Cass said blithely. And then she added with a sly grin, "Well, there are winners and then there are . . . *losers*." As she said it, her brown-black eyes swept through the shadows to include Sarah and her four closest friends.

Sarah shivered.

"You cold?" Riley White, sitting next to her, asked. "Want my sweater?"

Unsmiling, Sarah shook her head no. Smile or no smile, Riley was a friend of Cass's and could be, for all she knew, every bit as treacherous as their hostess, who had come up with this cruel game at her stupid party! Why had she ever let Maggie talk her into coming tonight?

"Morgan," Cass told a thin, red-haired girl in a pink dress standing just inside the door, "take . . ." She looked at Ellie and asked, "What was your name again? So many guests . . ."

Sarah made a face of distaste.

"Ellie," came the soft answer.

"Oh, yes, Allie, that's right. Morgan take Allie here and give her that consolation prize I told you about. Take your flashlight. It's on the table beside the door. While you're gone, the rest of us will get on with our fun and games. Go with Morgan, Allie. She has a nice prize for you. See you later."

Ellie shot Sarah a confused glance. But the girl with red hair came over and took Ellie's arm. "C'mon," she said impatiently. "I haven't got all day!"

As Ellie hesitantly followed Morgan from the room, a blonde girl opposite Sarah murmured, "My grandmother has a dress just like that!" and giggled.

Sarah knew Ellie had heard, because her head jerked up, her shoulders stiffened and, although her cheeks were scarlet, she left the room with her head held high.

Good for you, Ellie! Sarah applauded silently. She shot the blonde girl an icy look and fantasized about stealing a chair right out from under her in the final round of the game.

But when Shane lost during the next round and

was promptly led away by another of Cass's "assistants," this one a tall, dark-haired girl, and then Donald found himself without a chair in the third round, Sarah realized that no matter how quick and agile she might be, she was *not* going to emerge triumphant in this game.

Because it was clear that when Cassandra Rockham had said five people would be losers, she had been talking about Sarah Drew and her four best friends. I was wrong, Sarah thought, thinking that Cass wouldn't know who was going to lose. The only time her finger presses down on the Stop button is when one of us is rounding a corner and can't possibly grab a chair in time.

Providing losers for this game couldn't be the only reason they'd been invited to this party, Sarah thought nervously. That was a ridiculous idea. Cass had plenty of guests who could have failed to grab a chair when the music stopped. She wouldn't have invited a group of five strangers solely for that purpose.

Sarah felt her stomach recoil. Did that mean there was more in store for them?

What . . . was . . . going . . . *on*?

And why hadn't Ellie returned?

Whatever it was that was happening, Sarah was certain that she or Maggie would be the next person minus a chair.

She tried in vain to catch Maggie's attention. But, cheeks flushed, eyes bright, her best friend was concentrating totally on the game. Sarah could see

44

how determined Maggie Delaney was to avoid being the next person to leave the room.

She might as well relax, Sarah thought grimly as Cass's hand pushed a button and the music stopped. If I lose in this round, Maggie is sure to lose in the next one. We're the only two left from our group.

It was Maggie who got caught when the music stopped. Sarah, watching Cass carefully, saw her finger poised over the button, saw it go down the second that Maggie reached the end of the column of chairs. There was no question in Sarah's mind that the motion was precisely timed for Maggie's arrival at that particular place.

But why?

Disappointment showed on Maggie's face. But, always the good sport, she shrugged good-naturedly and followed Morgan out of the room.

Sarah glared at Cass. Ellie should be back by now. Donald and Shane were still missing, too. Cass had made it sound as if the "consolation prizes" were nearby. So why hadn't any of her friends returned yet? And how was Sarah going to find them in such a huge house without lights when this stupid game was over?

She knew one thing for sure. The very second she did find her friends, they were leaving, whether Maggie liked it or not. They'd obviously been invited for a reason, and simply losing at this game couldn't be all of it. There was more ahead of them, and Sarah was sure that whatever Cass had in mind for her and her friends, it wasn't good.

They weren't going to hang around and find out
what that something was. Not if Sarah Elizabeth
Drew had anything to say about it!

She wasn't the least bit surprised when she found
herself without an available chair the next time the
music stopped abruptly.

With one thoroughly disgusted glance in Cass's
direction and an annoyed look at Riley White, who
looked mildly puzzled, Sarah followed Morgan out
of the room.

Chapter 7

Watching the small, thin, red-haired girl striding confidently ahead of her in spite of the near-darkness, Ellie felt like an awkward bulky green lump in high heels. What was it like to move so effortlessly, so lightly? Did this girl in front of her work out daily? How did someone stay that thin? She had probably never touched a chocolate milk shake in her entire life.

"Where are we going?" Ellie asked timidly. She couldn't see very well. Morgan was being very selfish with the flashlight, keeping it too far in front of Ellie to do her any good.

They seemed to have been walking for a long time. Why were Cass's "consolation prizes" so far away from the party?

"Hurry up!" came the impatient answer. "You're so slow!"

Flushing with shame, Ellie tried to quicken her steps. But she seldom wore high heels and was unsure in them. She tripped and would have fallen if

Morgan hadn't heard her gasp. She turned to grab Ellie's arm and haul her upright.

Suddenly irritated, Ellie thought, What are we doing outside in the first place? This path is full of little stones and it's hard to walk. Anyway, the party's *inside*.

Instead of thanking Morgan for saving her from a bad fall, Ellie said abruptly, "I want to go back to the party. I don't need a prize. I just want to go back and find my friends." Ellie had attended very few parties, but the ones she had attended had never included being whisked away before the festivities got underway. Something was very weird here.

"Sorry," Morgan said, moving on. "I have my orders. I have to take you where Cass told me to. C'mon, we're almost there. I wish you'd hurry *up!*"

Defiance was not one of Ellie's qualities. She continued to follow Morgan. But she was becoming a little frightened by what was happening to her. Were all big, sophisticated parties like this? Everything that had happened so far seemed so . . . *weird*. But she didn't want to admit that she wasn't having a good time. That would be proving Ruth right. She couldn't stand the thought of that.

Because if Ruth had been right about that, she might have been right about all of it. Ellie might actually have been banished from the party because she didn't deserve to be there in the first place. Maybe Cass had noticed right away that Ellie didn't belong. Maybe she'd realized that she'd made a big mistake inviting Ellie and had quickly set about correcting that mistake. So her finger had pressed the STOP button at the exact instant when Ellie couldn't possibly grab a chair.

If Ruth had been right, then Cass had arranged for Ellie to lose at musical chairs not only to get her out of the room, but to get her out of the *house*, far from the party she'd been so excited about.

Tears of misery filled Ellie's blue eyes.

It was very dark outside with no moon. The predicted cold front had arrived, turning the warmth of an Indian-summerlike day into a more typical chilly autumn evening. The path Morgan followed was rough, dotted with small stones and sticks, and there were strange noises coming from the woods on both sides of the path.

Ellie, defiant or not, decided she'd had enough and was trying to summon up enough courage to say so, when Morgan announced, "Here we are! This is your spot."

Her spot? What did *that* mean?

"I want to go back to the party," Ellie said again, more bravely this time. "I don't want to be out here. Take me back!" She hoped Morgan hadn't detected the fear in her voice. She might make fun of Ellie. Ellie couldn't stand that on top of everything else.

Ignoring Ellie's demand, Morgan urged, "Oh, go on in! Cass is in there, waiting for you. She took a short-cut to beat us here. She's got a surprise for you. Go ahead!"

Ellie hesitated. A surprise? For her?

But there was something in the red-haired girl's voice . . . something artificial. Like Ruth's, when she had told Ellie there was a "treasure" hidden in the basement. Then, when Ellie had fallen for the ruse and ventured into the damp, dark cellar, Ruth had slammed the upstairs door and locked it.

Morgan's voice held that same fake quality.

I'm being paranoid, Ellie told herself. Cass isn't Ruth and neither is Morgan. This is a party and parties are full of games and surprises, aren't they? If I'm going to have a good time, I have to get into the spirit of things. If Morgan is telling the truth, then Cass wasn't trying to get rid of me. She was *including* me, in some kind of special game.

Hesitantly, but with her head up and a tentative half-smile on her face, Ellie stepped inside the door Morgan held open for her.

It was dark inside. She couldn't see much, and she hesitated just beyond the threshold. The room *felt* empty. But she waited for Cass to flood the room with light and shout, "Surprise!"

When that didn't happen, Ellie turned back toward Morgan. "Where — " she began.

But her question was interrupted by the forceful slam of the door in her face. Startled, Ellie stepped to the door, reached for the knob to pull it open.

And heard the unmistakable sound of a key turning in the lock.

Shane had no intention of following the dark-haired girl in the too-tight purple dress any further than out of the room. When they reached the foyer, she would escape her "guide" and bolt for the front door.

She never should have come. She didn't belong here. It was too creepy. Not at all like a party. It was too dark, too quiet, too . . . bizarre. She'd never attended a party like this one, and she didn't want to ever again. Cass had a strange idea about what "festive" meant.

She had to get out of this place.

And this silly, childish game of musical chairs had given her the perfect opportunity.

But when they left the room and entered the crowded, shadowed entry hall, the girl in purple closed amazingly strong fingers around Shane's left wrist and said, "Not that way. *This* way!" and began tugging Shane toward the wide, curving staircase.

A deeply ingrained horror of calling attention to herself in a crowd forced Shane away from the relief of the front door and up the stairs with her companion, who hadn't released her grip. Better to go with the girl and figure out another way to leave than cause a fuss and make everyone stare at her. She couldn't bear that.

She'd had enough of that in Rockport to last a lifetime.

After several silent minutes of climbing stairs, Shane asked the girl the same question that Ellie had asked. "Where are you taking me?"

She received no answer.

Tiny butterflies of unease began fluttering inside Shane. Maybe she should have left when she had the chance.

After a few minutes, they reached a tall, white, panelled door. While the girl in purple was bending to insert a key, Shane noticed something peculiar. Next to the door was a roll of small round orange stickers hanging on the wall. Not the sort of thing she expected to see in a beautifully-decorated mansion.

Strange.

The door opened, and the girl stepped inside. "C'mon in," she said without a smile. "Your prize package is in here. When you've opened it, you can come back to the party. I have to get back now."

Shane had no intention of returning to the party. Ever. Still, she'd let the girl think she did. It was easier that way. She'd just slip out as soon as the girl had gone back downstairs.

But as Shane moved into the room — a wide, low-ceilinged space with a few lighted candles scattered about and a set of double French doors in the center of the far wall — the girl whipped around and left the room so swiftly that Shane felt a breeze.

In the next split second, the door closed, a key turned, and Shane's heart stopped. Locked in? No! No, she couldn't be! It wasn't possible. She hadn't done anything wrong.

Praying frantically that she was mistaken, Shane raced to the door and grasped the knob. She turned it. Nothing happened. The door was immovable.

She shook the knob, twisted it, pushed hard on the door. Still nothing. She began pounding on it with her fists, shouting, "Open this door! Open it right now! Let me out of here!"

There was no response. Only silence.

Shaking, stunned, and disbelieving, Shane stood

frozen, facing the solid slab of wood that held her prisoner.

This . . . couldn't . . . be happening.

It couldn't. But it was.

Donald wouldn't have minded leaving the room when he lost at musical chairs if Maggie had come with him. She looked so pretty tonight. But then, when didn't she?

Following his guide, he told himself they still had the whole night ahead of them. He'd collect his prize and then beat it back to Maggie. The game would probably be over by then and they'd have the rest of the evening to party.

Personally, if *he* were having a party, he wouldn't include a babyish game like musical chairs. He would have thought that Cass was too sophisticated for such a silly game.

You never could tell about people.

His guide opened a door and gestured Donald inside. In the pale yellow glow of her flashlight he could see that the room they'd entered was huge and filled with expensive furniture. Antiques, maybe. The walls were covered with silver foil, like Christmas wrapping paper, and the carpet was soft and thick under his feet.

A set of folding doors stood half open at his elbow.

"In there," the girl, a thin redhead, said curtly. She had led Ellie away first and then, after someone else took Shane away, she'd come back for him. She was still a little out-of-breath from hurrying. "Your prize is in the closet," she said, pointing toward the double doors. "You can get it yourself."

Impatient to return to Maggie, Donald stepped inside.

It was dark, as he'd expected. What he hadn't expected was the sight of a video camera, high up on the wall, its round unblinking eye looking down upon him. An avid camera buff, Donald was wishing he could reach the videocam to take a better look at it, when the big double doors suddenly snapped shut.

"Hey, what — ?" he began, whirling around in surprise to face the doors.

The sound of fumbling on the other side increased his suspicion.

"What's going on?" he called loudly. "What are you doing out there?"

There was no answer.

But when he began pushing on the doors, tentatively at first, then more forcefully, nothing happened. They didn't give an inch.

It wasn't until Donald had finally given up, completely understanding that the doors were *not* going to open, that he remembered what had caught his attention when they'd first entered the room. He had noticed it because it seemed so totally out-of-place in a perfectly coordinated room.

Directly outside the folding doors, pinned onto the silver foil wallpaper, had been a roll of bright pink small round stickers. Thinking only that the rich had strange tastes, he'd dismissed the odd sight, believing that it had nothing to do with him.

Now, he wasn't so sure.

Maybe, in view of this weird party, its bizarre game, and now his being held captive in a closet, maybe that roll of stickers did have something to do with him.

But what?

Maggie didn't like being ordered around as if she were someone's servant. The only reason she continued to follow Cass's lackey was that Donald had, too. She believed her guide was taking her straight to Donald and Ellie and Shane.

But the narrow little room her guide pointed out to her was empty.

"Where — ?" Maggie began, but before she had finished the question, the girl was gone, the door clicked shut after her, and a lock snapped into place.

Maggie was alone.

Threading her way through the noisy crowd gathered in the entry hall, Morgan led Sarah up a wide, winding staircase to the second floor and then down a long hallway carpeted in beige. Their high heels made absolutely no sound as they moved along the white-walled corridor.

"Where on earth are we going?" Sarah demanded, annoyed. "Are my friends going to be there?"

No answer from Morgan, who continued on down the hall to its end, where she stopped and pushed open a heavy wooden door.

"In here!" she said curtly. "Hurry up! I have to get back."

Sarah wasn't about to enter any room in Cass's house without checking it out first. Not at a party as strange as this one was turning out to be.

But, as she hesitated on the threshold, peering inside, Morgan let out an exasperated sigh. And a second later, a hand between Sarah's shoulder blades sent her stumbling into the room. Unprepared, she lost her balance and fell to the floor. The door slammed shut behind her and there was the sound of a key turning in the lock.

Sarah had no idea where she was or what she was doing there. But she knew, with sickening certainty, that the door would not open when she tried to turn the knob.

She was a prisoner.

Chapter 8

"Okay," Cass announced when Sarah had left the room, "game's over! We're going to do something else now. Let's put all the chairs back and you can grab something to eat if you want to before we start the new game."

"What about the people who left the room?" Riley White asked as people began replacing the chairs along the walls. "Shouldn't they be back by now?"

Cass smiled and turned to take a cup of punch from the buffet table behind her. "Relax, Riley. You'll find out in a minute. Help Morgan put those chairs along the wall, will you?"

When order had been restored to the room, Cass stood in front of her guests and pushed a button on a panel beside her. Immediately, the rock group on the television screen at the front of the room disappeared.

"Now for our new game," Cass said. "Watch the screen, please. There are other sets in all the other rooms and on the terraces, so everyone can see." She pressed another button on the panel.

Instantly, the screen filled with the broad, plain face of Eleanor Whittier. She looked totally bewildered. She was slowly turning her head from side to side, apparently examining her surroundings.

Cass pressed the button again. Eleanor's face disappeared. It was replaced an instant later by Shane's delicate features. Her pale blue eyes were wide with barely controlled panic. She seemed to be breathing through her mouth, as if she were struggling for air. She was obviously terrified.

Someone whispered, "Wow! That girl is losing it!"

Ignoring the comment, Cass continued pushing the buttons.

Donald's thin, angled face filled the screen. His lips moved and although there was no sound, viewers could almost hear him saying slowly, "What the heck . . . ?" There was no fear in his voice, only confusion.

Maggie Delaney's face, when it appeared immediately after Donald's, showed only anger. Her lips were clamped together tightly, and her eyes were narrowed.

Sarah's face was the last to fill the screen. And, as with Maggie's, there was no mistaking the expression on the tanned, oval face. Sarah Elizabeth Drew was furious. Her nostrils flared with anger, her brown eyes glowed with fury.

Because each picture had been a close-up view of the missing guests, no clue as to their whereabouts had been visible on the screen.

Which, as Cass made clear a moment later, was the idea.

With a glint in her dark eyes, she said, "We're going to have a *people* hunt!"

While she waited for a reaction to this dramatic announcement, the screen continued to repeat the display of the missing guests' faces in order of their disappearance.

Reaching out once again to the panel, Cass switched on an intercom that sent her voice echoing throughout the mansion.

"Listen up, everyone," she called, "this is your hostess speaking. Quit partying and pay attention!"

After waiting a moment to make sure she was being heeded, Cass continued. "This party is going to be a little different. We're going to have a very special . . . 'treasure' hunt! We're going to hunt for the people whose faces you see on the screens in every room. It'll be a blast!"

There were a few murmurs from the crowd, but no one said anything aloud. Riley White was frowning, his arms folded against his chest. But he continued to listen carefully to Cass's words.

"There are two sets of cards to help you," she continued, holding up two thick, rubber-banded bundles of small cardboard rectangles. "One set is yellow. The other is white. I'll give some to everyone, along with small disposable flashlights." She beamed at her guests and added brightly, "See? I've thought of everything!"

Riley's frown deepened.

"The yellow cards will give you clues about where the five people are hidden. You'll have to figure out what each clue means." Cass laughed. Her thick dark hair moved against her cheeks. "They're not that hard, trust me."

Someone behind Riley groaned. "Sounds like a test to me. We get enough of this kind of stuff in school. I thought this was a party."

Ignoring the complaint, Cass went on with her explanation. "The second batch of cards, the white ones, have five little boxes outlined in black. At each of the five hiding places, which are all in the house or out on the grounds somewhere, there is a roll of stickers on the wall, each in a different color. When you find a hiding place, peel one sticker off the roll and put it on one of the boxes on your white card. The first person who comes back with all five stickers wins a big, fat gift certificate to the music store in the mall." Cass took a deep, satisfied breath. "Everyone got that?"

The blonde girl who had commented on Eleanor's dress said, "Not me! *I* don't get it. When we figure out the clues and find these people, are we supposed to bring them back with us?"

"No, of course not!" Cass answered sharply. "That would ruin the game. Leave them exactly where they are. Just bring me the stickers."

"Then it's not a people hunt," the girl answered with a pout. "It's just a stupid *sticker* hunt!"

"Look," Cass explained in a bored voice, "if you brought the person back with you, then no one else would get to find them! The game would be over too fast that way. It would be spoiled. Making you collect all five stickers is a better idea."

Riley stepped forward. "What makes you think all five of those people want to stay where you put them?"

"Who cares what *they* want? They can't leave, silly! Give me *some* credit for brains, Riley. They're locked in, of course."

Riley's mouth fell open. He stared at Cass. "You've got five of your guests locked up? Are you *nuts*? Cass, that's against the law, for Pete's sake, not to mention it being disgusting!"

Cass waved a hand in dismissal. "Oh, lighten up, Riley! Where's your sense of humor? This is a party! It's only for a little while, anyway, and I didn't put them in horrible places. They're not tied up or gagged or anything. They're fine."

The look of disbelief remained on Riley's face. "You're kidding, right? You invited five people here and now you're holding them prisoner? What's *wrong* with you? This isn't funny, Cass."

"Oh, stop looking at me like I'm a criminal and you're the judge. They'll think it's a hoot, wait and see. And if they don't," Cass added with a shrug, "it's no great loss." She laughed. "I just won't invite them next year."

Riley's mouth tightened. "This is the only reason you invited them, isn't it? To use them in this stupid game. Because you wouldn't have dared try it with your own crowd."

"You're *part* of that crowd, Riley," Cass reminded him tartly.

Riley stood up very straight, his mouth grim. "Cass, tell me something: Did these guys know ahead of time that they were invited as part of the entertainment?" Before Cass could answer he added, looking up at Sarah's angry face on the television screen, "I'd say from the look on that girl's face that they didn't." He shook his head in disgust. "What a crummy idea, Cass. Forget it! I'm not doing any people hunting!"

To Cass's annoyance, others in the room began echoing Riley's objections to the new game. Cries of "Too weird!" and "Get real, Cass!" reached her ears.

But there were always people eager to do Cass's bidding, and in no time at all she was surrounded by guests, small, pastel-colored flashlights in hand, clamoring for the little packets of cards, anxious to begin the hunt. People came from other rooms to ask for cards, teasing Cass for hints about the locations of the hidden guests, which she smilingly refused to give.

"You've got your clues, " she pointed out, "and now you're on your own. Better get going if you want to be the first one back here with a card full of stickers."

When most of the crowd had dispersed, cards in hand, Riley advanced toward Cass. "You can't be serious about this. Those five — " glancing toward the screen.

"Oh, relax!" Cass regarded Riley with mocking eyes. "None of them is the least bit important. Actually, I'm doing those nobodies a big favor. No one would even know they were *here* if I hadn't let them star in my little game. They should thank me." She smiled slyly. "What's the matter, Riley, afraid you won't win?"

Then, still smiling, she turned and flounced out of the room.

Alone, Riley stared down at the packets of cards in his hands. Then he glanced up at the screen. The furious face of a girl with reddish hair glared down at him. A drum majorette with the marching band, wasn't she? Delahanty? Delaney? She looked like she was ready to kill someone. Cass. He couldn't blame the girl, and if she wanted assistance, he'd be happy to give it.

Someone had to get those five out of their hiding places. Bending his dark head, Riley began studying the first of the yellow clue cards.

Chapter 9

The first thing Sarah noticed as she pulled herself to her feet was the horrendous noise that had begun when Morgan turned the key in the lock. She was surrounded by heavy-metal rock music, a sound she despised. It seemed to be pouring from every inch of the walls surrounding her. It was brutal. She had to stop it.

Pulling herself to her feet, Sarah peered into the darkness, her eyes searching for a stereo, a CD player, a radio, anything that might be responsible for the ear-shattering din. Shielding her ears with her hands to protect her hearing, she stumbled about the room, feeling with her feet for barriers.

The terrible crashing and pounding of instruments continued. It filled every corner, every crevice of the room. Sarah felt as if she were being beaten with rocks.

"I'll kill you, Cass Rockham!" she muttered as she tripped over something metal and fell against a table, cracking her cheek on hardwood.

If she ever got out of this nightmare. . . .

When, in rapid succession, she bumped into two metal racks standing on the floor, sending them clanging against each other like cymbals, and then into the bulky form of a grand piano, followed by a collision with a set of drums, she realized that the metal stands were music racks and she was in a music room.

Sarah made a sound of disgust low in her throat. A music room! How appropriate! In a brittle voice, Sarah said aloud, "Cass must know more about her guests than I thought."

But if Cass knew that Sarah was a musician, pumping this heavy-metal garbage into the room where she was being held prisoner was about as mean as a person could get, Sarah thought.

Her head aching from the horrible noise, Sarah leaned against the door, staring blankly out into the room. She had spent many hours in one kind of music room or another. Never once had it crossed her mind that such a place could be frightening. But this one was.

Get a grip, Sarah! she told herself, and began looking for a way out.

The room was windowless, probably, she thought, to protect the instruments from the hot rays of the sun or the chill of a blustery winter day, and she was sure it was also soundproof. So she couldn't open a window and climb out, and screaming would do her no good at all.

Searching for a light switch, Sarah discovered an

intercom unit. Relief washed over her. If her voice could be carried to another room, someone would come and let her out.

But when she flipped the switch, nothing happened. She flipped it five times, using a harsher motion each time. Still nothing happened.

The wires had been disconnected.

Discouraged and depressed, the discordant sounds crashing against her pained ears, Sarah sat down on the carpet.

"If only I could pass this all off as a joke," she said into the darkness. "A gag, a dumb game Cass dreamed up. Donald would. Ellie would, too, because anything worse would be unthinkable to Ellie, who had been so happy about being invited to this . . . this nightmare!"

As for Maggie, it wouldn't make any difference — joke or not, she'd be furious if she were, like Sarah, locked up somewhere.

But Sarah felt something deeper than simple fury. The bad feeling she'd had right from the beginning about this night was growing inside her. It clung to her no matter how hard she tried to shake it off. None of what was happening could be accidental. It had all been planned. Carefully planned.

But why? Why would Cass do this to her?

She had never done anything to Cassandra Rockham.

And what about Sarah's friends? Where were they?

* * *

Maggie was pacing back and forth in the narrow, tunnellike room where Morgan had taken her, her heels playing a staccato on the white tile floor. The tall, skinny space was illuminated by fluorescent tubing overhead. On either side of her were floor-to-ceiling shelves stocked with boxes and cans and jars and bottles of food and household supplies.

At least she wouldn't starve if Cass forgot about her in this strange little cubbyhole. There was enough food here, including bottled water, to keep a family of five fed for a year.

Maggie fought fear with all her might. She didn't frighten easily. With three brothers, she was used to practical jokes. Wasn't that what this was? It couldn't be anything more than that, could it?

Still, it was a *stupid* joke. And cruel. Asking people to a party and then yanking them away from it. She'd always known Cass was mean. Everyone knew it. But kidnapping? Locking people into little rooms? That was too crummy for words.

Maggie had tried the door half a dozen times after Morgan left, positive that it was simply stuck. But she'd finally had to face the truth: The door was firmly locked against her.

When I get back upstairs, Maggie told herself as her black heels *rat-a-tat-tatted* back and forth in the narrow space, I'm going to yank every inch of that shiny black hair out of Cass's spoiled, mean head. And I'd like to see anybody stop me!

A sound behind her stopped her in her tracks. The door! It was opening. Someone was coming to get her!

Well, that hadn't been so bad. She'd only been locked in for maybe five minutes. She still had the rest of the night to party. *After* she found Donald.

Maybe she'd leave Cass's hair alone. Why ruin the whole evening because of some cruel, stupid prank?

Bending to pick up her clutch bag from the floor where she'd placed it, Maggie was about to turn around and give her rescuer a grateful smile of thanks when, without warning, an arm came from behind her, encircling her neck in an iron grip, and something soft was thrust into her mouth, gagging her.

She had no chance to cry out or fight back.

In the next second, Maggie was shoved up against the shelves, a knee forcefully planted on her back, her face squashed into a row of cereal boxes as a rough, scratchy rope was wound around her hands, pinned behind her back.

Suddenly she was being dragged backward, propelled by the arm around her neck. Struggling frantically against the painful grip, Maggie was yanked along the narrow corridor, to the open steel door, up stone steps, out a side door into a dark, deserted area beside the house, and then up a grassy slope leading away from the mansion.

She could hear rock music and laughter from inside. She tried desperately to scream, to shout, to cry out for help. But the gag smothered her sounds.

Still kicking, still struggling, she was half pulled, half dragged up the hill some distance, and the party sounds gradually faded away.

It was very dark outside with no moon. There were no floodlights this far from the house. Maggie's eyes searched the darkness wildly for help, but she saw nothing, nobody.

Her attacker made no sound.

Maggie struggled to think. Fear was engulfing her in heavy black waves. She had to fight it. If she panicked, she didn't stand a chance.

Cass? Was it Cass dragging her away from the party? Who else would know where Morgan had taken her?

It wasn't Morgan dragging her, Maggie was positive of that. Morgan was a tiny person.

But Cass wasn't.

The air was cool, and Maggie's black dress had no sleeves. But the goosebumps raised on her arms were not there because of the night air, she knew that. They were there because she was, now, very afraid. More frightened than she had ever been in her life.

This was no practical joke. The viselike grip on her neck, the shove into the shelves, the harsh rope around her wrists, the evil gag in her mouth, the humiliation of being dragged against her will. This person meant her serious harm.

She had never felt so helpless.

They reached the top of the hill and crossed a wide stretch of cement that Maggie decided was probably a driveway. A huge wooden building loomed above them in the dark. A garage?

Maggie's attacker yanked open a small door in the side of the building. Then, holding herself as stiff and unyielding as possible, she was thrust inside.

The smell of gasoline mingled with stale air assaulted her nostrils as she plunged into deeper darkness. So she'd been right. It *was* a garage. Windowless, pitch-black, and chilly. She could barely make out the dark, heavy shapes of two or three large cars.

The inside of the garage was as black and cold as a tomb.

Maggie shivered.

Her captor shoved her roughly up against the rear door of one of the sedans, while opening the front door on the driver's side.

Maggie felt tears of frustration, anger, and fear stinging her eyelids. She couldn't bear to give her attacker the satisfaction of seeing her crumble. But she was so very, very scared. . . .

If the horrible gag were removed somehow, so she could scream, would anyone hear her?

Maggie thought, No, they wouldn't, and a terrible sense of isolation rose within her. She kicked out wildly, but it did no good. Before she realized what was happening she was lifted under the arms and tossed bodily into the car, landing in a heap, facedown on the front seat.

There was a fumbling sound behind her, near the steering wheel. In spite of her hands being bound behind her back, Maggie struggled upright and scrambled backward until she was squeezed against the passenger's door. She searched with her fingers for a door handle. If she could push the door open and throw herself out of the car, maybe she could escape. . . .

There was no door or window handle. Her searching fingers found only holes where the handles had been. They had been removed.

How could she get out of the car with no way to open the doors or windows? And the windows were only open a crack.

A harsh, guttural laugh echoed in her ears. It came from the same area where the fumbling was going on, near the steering wheel. What was happening?

Maggie shrank further away from the sound, squeezing herself against the door. What was her captor doing? Something horrible, she knew that. Something she'd never dreamed of in her wildest nightmares was happening here.

And she didn't know how to stop it.

Maggie sat paralyzed, frozen in terror, struggling to think clearly.

Then the dark shape of her attacker grunted with satisfaction as the engine turned over and caught. It roared briefly before settling down to an ominous hum.

The shadowy figure pulled away, out of the car. A second later, the car door began to close.

Maggie flung herself at it, hoping to keep it from shutting. She managed only to crack her forehead on the sill as the door swung shut, imprisoning her.

While she half lay, half sat on the seat, reeling

with shock and fear, the figure disappeared into the darkness. She heard, rather than saw, the garage door open and shut. She was alone.

She had been left there to die.

In the mansion, the television screens throughout the house continued to display the faces of Sarah Drew and her four friends.

But when Donald Neeson's face vanished, Maggie Delaney's image failed to replace it. Instead, there was only blackness.

No one noticed.

Chapter 10

Held captive in the soundproof music room, Sarah felt as if her head was splitting. She knew she had to find a way out.

It was clear to her that Cass's only reason for inviting them was to trick them.

Was Riley White in on the gag, too? Remembering the smile he had sent her before the musical chairs game, Sarah felt tears of anger and frustration threatening.

No! These horrible people weren't going to make her cry. "What am I *doing* here?" she cried aloud, getting up from the floor. I fell for that dumb invitation, just like Maggie and the others did.

Where *were* the others? If Cass had to isolate them from the party, why couldn't she at least have imprisoned them all together instead of separating them?

Sarah's anger stirred her to action. She still had her purse with her. Her wallet was in there. Hunting through its contents, she smiled grimly as she felt the cool, smooth plastic of a credit card.

Sarah had opened doors with credit cards before. Maggie's brother Sean had taught them how, because Maggie was constantly forgetting her keys and locking herself out of the house. It didn't always work. But it *had* to this time, Sarah thought.

It did work. As she left the room and closed the door firmly behind her, she let out a deep, satisfied breath.

Looking down the long, white hall, Sarah saw that it was empty. Party sounds echoed distantly along its length, but Cass had apparently posted no guards.

In a house this size, there had to be a back staircase.

There was. It, too, was unguarded, inviting Sarah to slip down it and escape.

Sarah hurried down the steps, out a side door, and in minutes was making her way along a grassy slope beside the mansion, on her way to the long, winding driveway and home, her violin and her mother's "I-told-you-so."

Although there were people hurrying along the lantern-lighted grounds, none paid any attention to the girl in the rust-colored dress heading purposefully down the slope. They seemed to be caught up in some kind of game, scurrying here and there, calling out to each other, using words that led Sarah to believe they were engaged in a hunt. Another one of Cass's idiotic games?

Her anger had carried her only as far as the edge of the lawn when uneasiness about leaving her friends took over. She didn't know the house and grounds and hadn't the faintest idea where to begin looking for the four . . . but she couldn't leave without them. At least, not until she was sure they were okay.

Biting her lip, Sarah whirled around and retraced her steps, hurrying back toward the house.

Eleanor Whittier had had ample reason in her lifetime to be unhappy — never being pretty enough, rich enough, or thin enough.

But she couldn't remember any time recently when she'd been more miserable than she was on this particular Saturday night — the same Saturday night that had earlier filled her with breathless anticipation.

Why had she been taken from the party and locked in this place?

What *was* this place? It was so dark. She couldn't see a thing. It smelled faintly like the barn on her grandmother's farm. She'd never liked the barn. It had spiders and, sometimes, bats.

But barns were big and wide and had high ceilings and huge doors. The door she'd come in was a regular door. A regular *locked* door, she reminded herself.

Why was she *here*? Why wasn't she at the party she'd been invited to attend?

It's because I look so awful in this dress, she thought despairingly. Cass took one look at me and knew I didn't belong. So she got rid of me.

Ellie, using her extended arms as a guide, felt her way through the darkness to a window. Even if she could get out somehow, she wasn't sure she could find her way back to the house. It was coal-black outside, and she had no flashlight. Without lights on in the mansion, how would she find it? They'd come an awfully long way through the woods.

"I'm *not* an outdoor person," Ellie wailed, sinking into a wide wooden chair behind a large shadowy rectangle she decided was a desk. "I don't want to get lost in the woods at night!"

Wouldn't Ruth just love to see her now? Tears began sliding down Ellie's round cheeks. Ruth would laugh her head off. "She said I'd have a terrible time, and she was right," Ellie murmured softly to herself. "I should have listened to her."

What kind of person *was* Cass Rockham, anyway, to invite people to a party and then hide them away, lock them up?

A terrible person. Mean, like Ruth. This was exactly the kind of "game" Ruth would dream up and find funny.

But Ruth wasn't *at* this party. She hadn't been invited.

A click from the direction of the door brought Ellie's head up. Someone was coming. And she was a mess!

Swiping at her tearstained cheeks with her hands, Ellie stood up, hope and expectancy flooding her face. She was being rescued. The game was over. And it hadn't been so terrible, after all. Now she could go find her friends and have the good time she'd expected since the invitation first arrived.

The door opened.

"Boy, am I glad to see you!" Ellie cried, hurrying forward through the darkness. "Thanks for coming to get me. I was beginning to go stir-crazy in here."

"No problem," her rescuer said with a smile. "Cass says you've been a really good sport. She wants to make it up to you. Just follow me, okay?"

Smiling with relief and gratitude, Ellie followed eagerly.

"Hey, Cass," a boy in the ballroom called to his hostess, who was dancing in the center of the room, "what's with the TV? There are only two faces up there now. What happened to the other three?"

Cass shrugged. "Who knows? The system probably got screwed up somewhere. Happens all the time. The cameras quit working and my dad throws a fit. It's no big deal. Forget about it!"

Chapter 11

Riley White, alone in a foyer alcove, studied the
first of five clues printed on the little yellow cards
in his hand.

> *Just hangin' around,*
> *Tie-in' one on,*
> *Creasin' my pants,*
> *Losin' my shirt,*
> *Shoe-in' everyone away!*

It made no sense. Riley shook the card angrily.
"Come on, dummy," he muttered, "figure it out!"
At this rate, it would take him all night to free all
five of the hidden guests. They must be going nuts,
wherever they were! How could Cass come up with
such a cruel "game"? He'd always known she was
selfish — but this time she'd gone too far.

Donald Neeson was thoroughly disgusted with
the way the party had begun. Here he was, stuck
in this dumb place, alone, and he hadn't even had

the chance to talk to Maggie yet! What a bust! Maybe Sarah had been right all along. Maybe they shouldn't have come.

The camera high up on the wall was driving him nuts. He hated being confined to small places, always had. But he couldn't panic because he was sure he was being filmed. That was probably Cass's joke: hide people and catch their reactions on film. Then Cass and all of her friends could sit around and watch people go bonkers. They'd probably think that was hilarious.

He felt like a fool. Cass's idea of a joke was sick! But he had only himself to blame. He should have known better than to think the five of them were really welcome at this party.

"You'll be sorry if you go to that party without me, Donald," Dolly had said on the phone.

Donald drew in a sharp breath of surprise. What had made him think of that? Dolly wasn't at this party. She wasn't even in town. She was in Willowcreek, half an hour away. Or was she?

When Sarah returned to the house, the level of noise had decreased. The crowd had thinned. She had passed several couples on her way up the steps. They were all holding something in their hands as they left the house and chattering about hiding places.

Sarah had ignored them. Whatever they were up to, she wasn't playing. All she wanted to do was find her friends and get away from this madhouse.

But by the time she reached the foyer, where

half a dozen couples were arguing over tiny yellow and white cards, her curiosity was overwhelming.

"What's going on?" she asked a boy in jeans and a blue sweater. "What's with the cards?"

"People hunt!" he shouted over the rock music and loud voices. "Up there, see?" He pointed to the television set situated high up on a wall. "That's our quarry."

Looking up, Sarah stared, uncomprehending. Shane's face, pale and frightened, stared out into space from the screen.

"Shane?" Sarah said slowly. "You're hunting for Shane?"

"I guess," the boy answered. "Don't know any of their names. Just their faces. We're supposed to figure out these clues, on these little cards here." He tapped the packet in his hands. "Boy, I'll tell you, they're tough! That Cass . . ."

Scarcely breathing, Sarah kept her eyes on the television set. Shane's face evaporated and Donald's appeared. He looked confused.

When his image faded away, there was only blackness.

"That's strange," the boy in the blue sweater said, frowning. "There's supposed to be five people up there, like there were before. Now there's only two. What happened to the other three?"

With sickening certainty, Sarah realized she was one of the missing three. *Her* face had been up there on that screen for everyone to see. Shame, embarrassment, and fury flooded her, making her knees weak. Cass had been *filming* them!

I saw a camera in the music room, she thought, but I never suspected . . .

Annoyance heavy in his voice, the boy said, "I'll bet somebody's letting those guys out. That's why there's nothing on the screen. I'd better find Cass and tell her someone's screwing things up. She said we weren't supposed to let anyone out, just collect the stickers. I hope the game's not ruined now."

Any other time, Sarah would have thought it funny that he was looking straight at her and didn't recognize her as one of the faces previously on the screen. He was too annoyed about having the game "ruined" to really look at Sarah.

But she couldn't find any humor in what was going on around her now.

Overhearing the boy's comment, a girl in a black dress standing behind Sarah said, "Cass already knows. She says the cameras are screwed up. Don't worry about it, that's what she said."

The boy shrugged in response. "Maybe. But I'm not going to keep playing if someone's letting those guys out. I'm going to find Cass and tell her to have someone check those cameras."

After the boy left, Sarah remained transfixed, her feet rooted to the black-and-white tiles. The only two faces appearing on the screen above her were Donald's and Shane's. Why not Ellie's? And where was Maggie's face? Were the cameras really not working? Or was there some other reason why all four of her friends weren't there?

I *know* why I'm not up there, Sarah thought.

Because I escaped. Did Ellie? And Maggie? If they did, where are they now?

Forcing herself to snap out of her shocked paralysis, Sarah tore her eyes from the set and glanced around the foyer. The crowd had thinned noticeably. She supposed they had gone off to "people hunt." The thought sickened her.

Spotting two small piles of yellow and white cards on a table underneath the television set, Sarah marched resolutely toward them. Picking up both piles, her eyes blazing with indignation, she quickly scanned them. She guessed that the black-lined boxes were where people were supposed to put the colored stickers, and turned her attention to the "clues."

They didn't look all that hard.

Okay. All right. This stupid, cruel game was already underway. She couldn't stop it. Too late for that.

What she *could* do was get to the hiding places and set her friends free. But . . . there was a problem. She wasn't worried about figuring out the clues. Cass might be rich, but she wasn't all that smart. Still, being able to figure out the clues wasn't enough. This house, these grounds, were completely unfamiliar to her. It would take her all night to find her friends.

It was then that, lifting her head, she spotted Riley White. Alone in a corner, his dark head was bent over packets of cards in his hands identical to the cards Sarah was holding.

Riley ran with Cass's crowd. He must know the property. Would he help her search?

Riley was just about to give up on the first printed clue and seek out Cass, forcing her to reveal all five hiding places when a husky voice behind him said, "It's a man's closet."

He turned to find the girl with the French braid, her eyes dark with anger, standing in front of him.

"How did you — ?" he began, about to ask her how she'd freed herself, but she didn't let him finish.

"See? *Hangin'* is hangers, then ties and shirts and pants and shoes . . . it's a man's closet. So it's probably upstairs. But," Sarah added firmly, looking directly into Riley's eyes, "I'm *not* playing this stupid game. I'm going to find my friends and let them out, and then we're leaving. Now that I know what Cass was up to, it makes me sick! So if all you want to do is collect stickers, do it with someone else, okay? But I need your help because I don't know my way around in this place, and I'd cut my throat before I'd ask Cass for help."

Sarah didn't know who was more surprised, her or Riley. She didn't make a practice of such outbursts.

But then, she didn't often find herself in a situation like this, either.

"I'm not playing," Riley said seriously, returning her direct gaze. "I intended to let them all out before you showed up. I hope you believe that. It's the truth."

Sarah hesitated. It didn't really matter whether

she believed him or not, did it? The important thing was finding her friends, not how she felt about Riley White.

But knowing that she had someone to help her in her search eased, slightly, the grim expression on her face.

"Well, then, what are we waiting for?" she said. "The closet must be upstairs. Let's go!"

Like Maggie, Donald breathed a sigh of relief when the sudden sound of a sharp hammering at the door startled him. He was sitting on the floor, trying to avoid the camera lens and suspecting he wasn't being all that successful when the hammering caught him by surprise.

Someone was coming to get him. Why didn't they just use a key?

The first thing he'd do when he was free was hunt for Maggie. Then they could spend the rest of the evening together. If that was okay with her. . . .

Donald never saw the person who tossed a black cloth over the videocam and then dealt him, from behind, a sharp blow on the temple.

He felt for one brief instant the sensation of being lifted, and then everything faded into black.

Shane couldn't shake the panic that threatened to overwhelm her. Locked in! She couldn't stand it! What had she done wrong? Why was Cass doing this to her?

And where were her friends?

There were windows in her hiding place, but only blackness lay beyond them. She hated the dark. It hid things. How could she know what to be careful of if she couldn't *see*?

Suddenly Shane could no longer control herself. Unseeing, unthinking, she ran to the door and attacked it, pounding on it with both fists and screaming for help until her fists were red and swollen and her throat burning.

No one came in answer to her cries.

Exhausted, Shane collapsed onto a small antique settee against the wall, curling up in a little ball on the maroon velvet cushions, shaking violently.

Chapter 12

In the garage, the car engine continued to hum ominously as Maggie fought rising panic. She had to get out of the car! For now, the deadly fumes spewing out of the exhaust pipe were spreading out through the huge garage. But soon enough, they would reach her. She couldn't wait for that to happen.

There had to be a way to call for help.

The horn . . . the car horn! Would a car horn, blasted repeatedly, be mistaken for party noise? Maybe not. Maybe someone would be out walking on the grounds and hear, and come rushing to help her.

Oh, please, she prayed, please. . . .

Her hands still tied behind her back, Maggie leaned forward over the steering wheel. Using her chin to locate the horn ring, she pressed down hard.

Nothing. Not a sound.

She would have to press harder. Drawing her head back, she took a deep breath and lurched forward, slamming her chin down full force on the horn ring. The impact sent pain shooting through her jaw and up into her already aching head, and she cried out.

But her muffled cry was the only sound she heard. The horn remained silent.

Maggie repeated her attack on the horn three more times before giving up. Her chin throbbed, her jaw ached, and her head rang with pain, but still the horn was silent as a grave.

A grave? Maggie shuddered.

The wires to the horn must have been disconnected.

How long did it take to die of carbon monoxide poisoning?

She did not want to die.

Sinking back against the seat, her eyes probed the shadows for something, anything, that she might use to tear the disgusting gag from her mouth. If she could scream, if she could call someone, there was still a chance that she would be heard and discovered in time.

The turn signal lever near the steering wheel beckoned to her through the shadows. If she could hook an edge of the rag around the lever and yank her head backward, maybe the motion would dislodge the rag.

In the dim interior of the car, Maggie maneuvered in the front seat. What if her plan didn't work?

At first, it didn't. It took several attempts at bending her head to the steering wheel before she managed to hook an end of the rag around the lever. And several more tries before the end stopped slipping off the lever when she yanked her head backward.

But finally, just as she was about to give up, she hooked an end of the rag around the lever and, praying softly to herself, jerked her head backward as fast as she could.

And this time it worked. The filthy rag clung to the lever and was yanked out of her mouth as the back of her head hit the seat.

Her mouth was free.

Maggie began screaming at the top of her lungs.

Shane examined her surroundings carefully. The French doors to her left might provide an escape. It was worth checking out. Better than staying here alone in this dim, silent, empty room.

She walked to the French doors and pulled one open.

Then, dizzy and pale, she gasped, stumbled backward, and quickly shoved the door closed.

It was not a way out. Not for *her*.

Riley and Sarah hurried up the stairs, oblivious to the couples lounging on the steps and against the railing, guests who had opted not to take part in the "people hunt."

"Good luck!" one boy called after them, and Sarah made a face of disgust. He approved of Cass's nasty game? Idiot! He was as bad as his hostess!

The two of them checked every lavish bedroom upstairs. It wasn't until they came to the end of one of the long hallways and entered a large, dimly lighted room, that they found what they'd been looking for: a roll of round, vivid pink stickers tacked onto the wall beside floor-to-ceiling louvered folding doors. Beside the stickers hung a small yellow card bearing the clue Sarah had deciphered.

"This is it!" she cried, and then in the next second, moaned in disappointment. "Oh, no! I don't believe this! Look, someone's broken the lock, and whoever was in here is gone."

The lock, a white plastic arrangement suitable for folding doors, hung like a broken wrist on one white knob.

"That's strange," Riley said. "No one was supposed to let anyone out. Cass made a point of that."

Sarah thought for a minute. "Maggie and Ellie . . ." she said slowly, ". . . their faces weren't on the screen downstairs. Maybe they got away, like I did. So maybe *they* found whoever was in here. Donald, or Shane. Maybe Maggie and Ellie found them and broke the lock. But then where are they? I don't think they would have gone home without finding me."

She was about to leave the closet when she noticed, above her head, a small, ragged scrap of black paper fluttering like a bat's wings. It was tacked to a square of black cloth draped carelessly over the television camera.

Frowning, Sarah reached up to pull the scrap of paper free. Something was printed on it in what looked like white chalk.

"Riley, look at this," she said, emerging from behind the folding doors. "What *is* this?"

They read the message together, aloud, *"Chill out, guys!"*

Sarah looked at Riley and groaned. "Another stupid game?" she cried. " 'Chill out' ? What does *that* mean?"

Riley had no answer.

Maggie's screaming brought no response. In a windowless garage, so far from the noisy mansion, her desperate cries for help went unheard.

The car's engine chugged away relentlessly. She was feeling sicker and sicker. And she had never been so frightened in her life.

"Please, please," she cried aloud, "please, please, please . . ."

There had to be a way to end the engine's murderous *chug-chugging*. It was the only way she was going to get out of the garage alive.

"Think, think!" she shouted to herself. "There has to be a way. You have to stop the engine. You can't die here. Not *here*, not like this!"

Squirming and wiggling, Maggie slid around on the front seat so that her back was facing the steering wheel. Arching backward and straining the bonds around her wrists, she felt with her fingers along the steel column.

And her fingernail caught, finally, in the small slot that was the ignition key's home.

But her probing fingers touched only emptiness. No key dangled from the slot.

"Oh, no," Maggie whispered, bitter disappointment mingling with fear, "no, no, no!"

The fumbling sounds she had heard had been her attacker hot-wiring the car.

Maggie's body collapsed forward into the seat, her face sinking into the rich leather upholstery. The urge to sleep was overwhelming.

Without an ignition key to turn off the deadly fumes, she had no chance. I am going to die, she realized.

With faint party sounds echoing distantly, Shane stood frozen in the center of a room gone almost completely dark. A night breeze had whooshed in through the open French door, dousing all of the candles but two on a table beneath a pair of antique dartboards. She was lost in a world of shadows.

Those doors were her only way out. But she couldn't bring herself to go near them.

"I can't," she murmured helplessly. "I can't!"

Something near her feet made a sound. A low throat-rumbling, half purr, half growl, it startled her and she stumbled backward.

A ball of fur emerged from underneath the table. Completely black, she would never have noticed the cat if it hadn't moved.

Relief at discovering she wasn't completely alone in her shadowy prison brought grateful tears to her eyes. "Kitty!" she cried. "Am I glad to see you!" She had a cat of her own, a white Siamese named Sophie. Sophie was sweet and affectionate, not as independent as some cats. She liked to be petted, and her favorite resting place was Shane's lap. Shane often felt that Sophie understood every word

Shane uttered and what's more, sympathized.

Even a cat who wasn't Sophie was better than nothing in this dark and scary isolation.

But her relief was short-lived. As she approached the animal, softly calling, "Here, kitty, kitty!" it arched its back and hissed menacingly.

Surprised, Shane halted, crouched close to the table.

The cat, its paw lifted threateningly, its claw extended, regarded her with narrow eyes turned a cold green-gold by the flickering candlelight.

"Oh, come on, kitty," Shane coaxed. "I won't hurt you. We're both trapped here, so we should be friends. Don't be scared. I'm scared enough for both of us. Be nice, okay? You're all I've got right now."

She edged closer, continuing to talk in a soft, gentle voice. Reaching out one hand, she attempted to stroke the black, velvety fur.

In the next instant, the sharp claws descended with dizzying speed and accuracy, slashing across her hand like razor blades.

Shane screamed in pain and fell backward, clutching her wounded hand. Blood began to seep up between the fingers of the protecting hand. When she lifted it, she stared in horror at the raw, bloody furrows.

Now she was unable to stop the tears that cascaded down her cheeks, slid off her chin, and began carelessly spotting the bright-red dress.

"Did you hear that?" a boy asked his girlfriend as they left the house to search the grounds for

Cass's hidden guests. "Sounded like a scream."

"It's a *party*, Keith," she replied, playing her pink flashlight along the ground in front of them. "Somebody probably just spilled punch on a two-hundred-dollar dress. Forget it. I *want* that gift certificate. Come on, Keith!"

Putting the scream out of his mind, Keith followed obediently.

Standing at the foot of the wide staircase, thoroughly disgusted with their failure to find anyone in the upstairs closet, Riley and Sarah studied a second yellow card.

A loaf of bread, a jug of wine

"What kind of stupid clue is that?" Riley complained.

"Ask your friend Cass!" Sarah said curtly. "This was *her* idea. And for all I know, you were in on it, too."

Riley raised his hands in mock self-defense. "Not me," he said. "I had *nothing* to do with this. You don't really think I'm like that, do you? The kind of weirdo who'd think it was a neat idea to lock people up at a party?"

"How should I know? I don't know anything about you except that you're a friend of the jerk who invited me and my friends. We never should have come," Sarah added heavily.

"Hey, don't say that." Riley's voice was gentle. "I'm glad you came." He put a hand on her shoulder.

"I'm really sorry all of this is happening. But I'm *not* sorry you're here. Otherwise, I might never have met you. And when everything's okay again, I'd like to do something about what you just said."

Sarah lifted her head. "About Cass being a jerk? I think it's too late to do anything about that. Besides, it's probably genetic."

Riley laughed. "No, I mean the part about you not knowing anything about me. That's the part I'd like to fix." Then, sensing Sarah's embarrassment, he added briskly, "Okay, now let's figure this out," and held up the yellow card. "Bread, wine . . . sounds like it could be the kitchen, right?"

Sarah nodded, trying to regain her composure. Riley's words had unsettled her further. He wanted to get to know her better? Any other time, that thought might have thrilled her. But she had her friends to think about now. She was too worried about them to think about romance.

"Right," Sarah said, "the kitchen. Let's go!" Then she stopped and looked up at him. "Just exactly where *is* the kitchen in this place?"

Looking pleased to be helpful, Riley took her hand and led the way.

Chapter 13

In the garage, Maggie felt weak and nauseated, and she knew time was running out.

But without an ignition key, there was no way to stop the engine and cut off the poisonous fumes.

Wriggling around again so that she was facing front, she peered out the windshield. The garage wall directly ahead of her was wooden. Not brick, or stone. The car, a heavy European sedan, could probably break through the wood.

"What's on the other side of that wall?" she murmured weakly. "Something soft and safe, like a field of grass? Or maybe a solid brick wall like the one at the entrance to this estate?"

Then, "What difference does it make what's on the other side of that wall? It's my only way out. And if I don't take it, if I stay in this garage, I'm dead."

When the sound of her own voice seemed to calm her, she continued her solitary conversation.

"I have to get out of here. Now! The engine of

this car is already running, so . . . where is the stupid gas pedal?"

Fumbling around on the floor with her feet, she located the pedal.

"Okay, here goes!" She pressed down on it, gunning the engine.

The car didn't move an inch.

"It's not in gear!" Maggie wailed. "If I just had a light so that I could see!" Then, "But even if I could, how can I shift into drive with my hands tied behind my back?"

She fought against tears of desperation. "Crying won't do any good," she scolded. "Think! *Think!*"

Maggie's stomach heaved with nausea, and her head ached. The desire to give up, to close her eyes and sink into blessed unconsciousness was a deadly trap, she knew that. She mustn't give in to it.

But if she didn't break free of the garage in the next few minutes, it would be too late. She would die in the car, in the garage, and her body wouldn't be found until long after the party she'd been so excited about.

There had to be a way to put the car in gear.

Riley and Sarah were prevented from entering the kitchen. A member of the catering staff stood guard at the door, saying firmly, "Kitchen's off limits, guys. No one's allowed in here but us."

"Cass would have known that," Riley pointed out to Sarah as they turned away, "so she wouldn't have hidden anyone in there. Whatever the clue about a loaf of bread and a jug of wine means, it's not the kitchen."

Sarah was already studying a second yellow card. "We'll have to leave that one for later. This one says, *To carry the sleigh*."

"Run that one by me again," Riley said.

"It's from that Thanksgiving song. You know, 'Over the river and through the woods'? That one. 'The horse knows the way to carry the sleigh . . .'"

"Oh. Horse?" Riley's brown eyes lit up with comprehension. "The stables! Got to be the stables. Come on! I've got a flashlight. Let's go!"

Grabbing Sarah's hand again, Riley hurried her outside.

Maggie, dizzy and sick, leaned forward to move her head around the steering wheel, searching for the shift lever. There was no clutch on the floor, only the gas and brake pedals, so she knew the car was an automatic. The lever should be on the steering wheel column somewhere.

"Where *are* you?" she cried. "You've got to be here!"

But only the turn signal lever brushed against her cheek.

"Where *is* it!" she screamed.

Then she remembered. It was a European car. The gear shift was on the floor between the seats. The short, squat lever had punched her in the stomach when she was first tossed onto the front seat. The blow had taken her breath away.

If her mind wasn't so foggy with fumes and panic, she'd have remembered right away.

But how to move the lever into drive with no hands?

"There's nothing wrong with my legs," she told the steering wheel angrily. She swivelled on the seat, brought her foot up and out and down against the lever, pushing with what little strength she had left.

The car jerked.

Maggie hesitated, struggling to concentrate. She couldn't see a thing. What if she shoved the lever into reverse instead of drive? She'd go zooming backward through the garage doors and careen down the steep hill, crashing herself and the car when she reached the bottom.

Even if she managed to shift the car into drive, the Olympic-sized swimming pool she'd heard so much about could be sitting right on the other side of the garage wall. The car would smash through the wall and sail into the pool, sink, and she would drown.

"But those are only *maybes*," she said into the dark emptiness. "Staying here, I'll definitely die."

Head spinning, heart thudding slowly in her chest, Maggie squeezed back against the seat, took a deep breath, and slammed her foot down on the gas pedal. Hard.

"Please," she prayed, "please . . ."

The car shot forward like a bullet, aiming itself straight for the garage wall.

When the car and the wall collided, splintering

boards and sending them flying through the air, Maggie was catapulted forward. Her head slammed down and against the steering wheel with a resounding crack.

She groaned and slipped into grateful unconsciousness as the expensive sedan found freedom in a grassy, open field beyond the garage. Slowed by the collision with the wall, it came to a gradual halt in the darkness.

Sarah and Riley, hurrying toward the stables, both heard the crash.

"What was that?" Sarah asked, stopping to tilt her head inquisitively.

"Came from out back," Riley said, pointing behind the garage. "We'd better check it out. Come on!"

They broke into a run.

When Ellie and her new guide arrived at a small redwood building deep in the woods instead of at the party house, the girl gestured Ellie inside.

Crushed by this new turn of events, Ellie protested. "I . . . I don't want to go in there! It's dark. There can't be anyone else in there. I thought you were taking me back to the party."

"Well, you thought wrong." The voice was unfamiliar and the guide, enveloped in a long, baggy coat and a large, floppy hat, unrecognizable. Ellie thought it was strange party gear. Much worse than her green dress! "This is where Cass wants you to wait for her."

Ellie hesitated. "Where are my friends?" she asked.

"How should I know? Listen, just go inside, okay? I have to get back to the party."

"No!" Ellie said stubbornly, surprising both of them. "I'm going back to the house. I want to find my friends. I don't *want* to go in there."

"Yes, you *do*!" came the angry response. Ellie, caught off guard, was pushed with full force through the open door. The hand between her shoulder blades sent her first to her knees on a smooth wooden floor. Then, unable to regain her balance, she tumbled forward, sprawling on her stomach, her arms splaying out helplessly in a futile effort to stop her fall.

And for the second time that evening, a door closed behind her. When she pushed against it, she found it wouldn't budge.

After a second or two of complete and deadly silence, Ellie put her face down on her arms and began to cry.

Chapter 14

The scene that greeted Riley and Sarah as they raced around a corner of the garage jolted them to a stunned halt.

A classic silver car sat nestled in a sea of grass, its engine running. Its route of escape from the garage was clearly visible in the golden arc of Riley's flashlight: The rear wall of the building boasted a huge, jagged hole, and broken white boards lay scattered about the field like matchsticks.

Only the steady hum of the engine sounded in the silence as the breathless pair slowly approached the car. Riley's flashlight traced a pale yellow pattern across the vehicle as they drew closer.

"Look," Sarah cried, tugging urgently on Riley's hand, "there's someone in the car! Who is it?"

Aiming his flashlight at the window on the driver's side, Riley answered after a moment, "It's that redhead, the drum majorette. One of your friends."

"Maggie?" Sarah gasped, rushing forward to peer in the window. "It's Maggie! Oh, God, she's hurt!"

Sarah reached down to open the door, only to discover that there were no door handles. There were gaping holes where the handles had been.

Someone hadn't wanted Maggie rescued. And had gone to a lot of trouble to see that she couldn't be.

"She might be dead in there," Sarah whispered, clutching Riley's sweater sleeve. She made a choking sound low in her throat and began pounding on the driver's window with both fists, frantically screaming, "Maggie! Maggie, wake up! Please, wake up!"

"She's not dead," Riley said firmly, gently grasping Sarah's wrists to stop her futile pounding on the glass. "She drove the car out here, didn't she? She had to be alive to do that. She probably just got knocked out when she blasted through that wall." There was admiration for Maggie in his voice. "Help me get her out of there. Grab a board."

Riley snatched up one of the broken boards lying in the field and began using it as a battering ram against the windshield on the passenger's side. Sobbing softly, her eyes blank with shock, Sarah did the same.

It took precious minutes for the safety glass to crack, splinter and collapse enough to allow Riley to push halfway in and haul a limp Maggie out over the hood.

Sarah helped, her breathing ragged, her hands moving in jerky, agitated motions. Standing beside the hood of the car, gasping for breath, she caught Maggie around the waist as Riley gently slid the unconscious girl toward her. Together, they placed Maggie on the damp grass. Then they knelt beside her. Riley picked up the flashlight, aiming it at the victim.

"She's breathing," Sarah gasped gratefully. "She's not dead! Thank God!" But then, "Riley, look at this! Her hands are tied behind her back!"

Her voice shook with fury as she hastily undid Maggie's bonds. "Look what your friend Cass has done. If we hadn't heard the crash, Maggie would be . . . would be . . . dead by now. God, I can't believe this is happening! Why would Cass *do* this to Maggie?"

Before Riley could answer, Maggie, revived by the fresh, cool air, began choking and gasping. And her eyes flew open. Sarah, crying and laughing at the same time, bent to hug her friend, saying Maggie's name over and over again.

It took Maggie a few moments to recognize her best friend. "Are you really here?" Maggie whispered at last, her voice hoarse from screaming. "Sarah? Am I still in one piece?"

Sarah tried to laugh. "Yes, Maggie," she said, squeezing her best friend's hand. "You're still very together, as always. What happened to you? How did you get in that car? Who tied you up? Did Cass do this to you?"

Another coughing spasm seized Maggie. When it subsided, she said, "I don't know. I don't know . . . *any*thing. I didn't see who it was."

"Was the garage your 'hiding place'?" Riley asked. "Is that where you were taken?"

Maggie shook her head. "No. That girl took me to a little place with lots of shelves full of food. In the basement, I think. We went down some steps, I remember." She struggled to sit up. Sarah and Riley reached out to help her. "Then someone caught me from behind. He stuffed something in my mouth and tied my hands behind my back. Then he dragged me up here and locked me in the car." She shuddered violently. Riley put his arm around her to keep her from toppling backward. "The smell made me sick," Maggie continued weakly. "Being locked in that car . . . I couldn't see anything. . . ." Her voice caught as she looked up at Sarah with widened eyes. "He took all the door handles off! I couldn't get out, Sarah! I tried, but I couldn't!"

Sarah nodded. "I know. I was afraid *we* wouldn't be able to get you out."

Maggie smiled gratefully. "But you did. Thanks. Both of you." Then her smile disappeared as she looked from Sarah to Riley and back to Sarah again. "What's going on? I mean, I thought it was just a game, so I wasn't scared at first, just mad. But when I was grabbed from behind . . . I knew it wasn't a game anymore." Struck by the horror of what had happened to her, Maggie fell silent.

She was interrupted by the sudden sweep of a flashlight's beam. A moment later, Cass appeared over the rise of the hill.

"What is going on here?" she demanded imperiously. She played her light over the scene. When the beam hit the garage wall with its yawning, jagged hole, she shrieked. "Oh, good grief, what have you done to the garage?" Then she saw the car. "And my dad's Jag! That's his favorite car. You've trashed it! Are you *nuts*?"

Furious, Sarah jumped to her feet. "*You* did this!" she raged, her face inches from Cass's. "You tried to kill my friend! She could have died locked in there!"

Cass stood her ground. "What are you talking about? I didn't put anyone in the garage. That wasn't on my list of hiding places. It's too far from the house. I don't know how your little friend got into that car. Maybe she was trying to steal it."

Before Sarah could reach out and smack Cass for her arrogance, the car chugged, coughed, chugged again, sputtered, and the engine died.

It had run out of gas.

Riley stood up. "Take it easy, Sarah," he said quietly. "We can't be sure Cass is behind this. She does some really stupid things, but I never thought of her as a killer. Why would she do this?" Turning to Cass, he said, "Look, there's something really crazy going on here. This girl was almost killed. Her hands were tied behind her back, she was gagged so she couldn't scream, and she was locked in a car with its engine running and the door handles removed, in a closed garage. If she wasn't as clever as she is, she'd be dead now."

Maggie managed a weak smile of pride.

"How come you're up here all alone?" Riley asked Cass. "You can't be the only person who heard the crash."

Cass shrugged. "I told everyone I'd take care of

it. They didn't want to leave the festivities, anyway. And I didn't want a crowd up here. But I never expected to find this mess! I thought it was just somebody trying to crash the party."

No one laughed at the play on words. Cass hadn't meant it to be funny.

"Know what I think, Riley?" Cass asked, annoyance in her voice. "I think you and your new little friend here," flicking a hand in Sarah's direction, "are trying to get even with me for my people hunt. I know you didn't like the idea, and I suppose she didn't, either." She shrugged. "But wrecking the garage and my father's car is overkill, don't you think? My game was perfectly harmless. Yours wasn't!"

"Cass," Riley persisted, "this is no game. This is serious. You've got one very dangerous guest at your party. And none of us knows who it is. Who would do something this crazy?"

"Well, I wouldn't," Cass said indignantly. "Why would I? I don't even *know* the girl."

Her voice shaking with rage, Sarah shouted, "Maggie could have died! Someone deliberately tried to kill her! If it wasn't you who locked her in that car, who *was* it? Did you make one of your friends do it?"

"Of course not! I haven't the slightest idea who did it. Someone she knows, probably. Maybe some jealous friend who wanted to come to the party and wasn't invited." Cass tossed her head.

Thoroughly enraged by Cass's callousness, Sarah sputtered, "Why is your stupid garage so far from your house? That's why no one heard Maggie screaming. You walk all the way up here to get your cars?"

Cass laughed harshly. "Oh, please! *We* don't get our cars. George does — our chauffeur. He lives over the garage. I gave him the night off. Good thing, too. He's old. Hearing the crash when your little friend here took off through the garage wall might have given him a heart attack."

Abruptly, the tone of Cass's voice changed. "Listen," she said coolly, "since she's okay now," waving carelessly toward Maggie, "I don't see why we have to make a big deal out of this. I'll tell George to have the garage and the car fixed before my parents get back in a couple of weeks. My dad never looks at the back of the garage, anyway. But if he knew about this, he'd ship me off to boarding school. Now," she added with a toss of her dark hair, "I've got to get back to my party."

And as the three watched, speechless, the party's hostess turned and teetered on spike heels back down the hill. Her flashlight created a golden path ahead of her as she went.

Maggie was the first to speak. "That . . . that witch!" she gasped. "I don't *believe* her! I could have been a log on the beach for all she cared. I — " her voice cracked — "I thought I was dying in there," she said, gesturing toward the damaged garage. "And *she's* going back to her party?" Exhausted by this outburst, Maggie leaned against the car that had nearly killed her and gulped in huge drinks of cool, fresh air.

"We have to call the police," Riley said flatly as he and Sarah helped Maggie to her feet. "You *were* almost killed."

Maggie shook her head. "I'm okay, honest. Just a little shaky. We can't waste time calling the police now. They'd be asking us questions for hours and we don't have any of the answers. Let's find Donald and the others first. I'll feel better when I know for sure that what happened to me isn't happening to them. Then we'll call the police, okay?"

"I don't know," Riley said doubtfully. "You look kind of green around the gills to me. I think you need an ambulance. We should call the paramedics *and* the police."

"Later," Maggie insisted firmly. "First, find Donald and Shane and Ellie."

"I think Maggie might be right," Sarah agreed. "Whoever did this will still be running around loose while we're trying to convince the police that this wasn't a joke. I think we should make sure the others are safe first."

"Are you sure you're okay?" Riley asked Maggie as they reached the bottom of the slope and proceeded across the smooth, thick lawn in the dark.

Maggie had an enormous goose egg on her forehead, her hands were scratched and dotted with tiny cuts from being pulled through the broken windshield, and her legs refused to hold her up without Riley's and Sarah's support. But she shook her head again and replied with absolute conviction, "I'm fine. Just find the others, *please!*" Her voice faded rapidly and began to shake as she added, "I'm scared for them. I'm really scared."

Neither Riley nor Sarah told her she was being silly.

Because they, too, were scared.

Chapter 15

"I wish I could come with you," Maggie said forlornly as Riley and Sarah led her to a sitting room off the front hall. "But I'd just slow you down. Come back and get me the second you find the other three, okay? Have you seen Donald at all, Sarah?" There was a note of halfhearted hope in her voice.

"Not since he lost at musical chairs. They stuck me in the music room upstairs, alone." Sarah managed a faint grin. "But thanks to your brother Sean, I didn't stay there very long."

Maggie returned the grin. "You had a credit card with you?"

Sarah nodded. Then she added seriously, "The only way we can find Donald, Shane, and Ellie is by figuring out those stupid clues of Cass's. And unless that maniac was only after *you*, Maggie, I think we'd better figure them out fast."

"Anyone could be a target, Sarah," Riley tried to reassure her. "We don't know that your friends are in any more danger than anyone else."

"Maybe not. But unless they've escaped, my

friends are the only ones who are *locked up* somewhere, alone. Which makes them sitting ducks."

Riley couldn't argue with that logic. It made sense.

"Cass has to be behind this," Maggie said. "She's the only one who knew where I was hidden."

"She might have told someone else," Riley said. "Maybe several someone elses. It really could be anybody."

That sobering thought plunged them all into a dark, despairing silence.

Before they left Maggie, Riley slipped out of his white sweater and insisted that she put it on. "My shirt has long sleeves, " he said when she protested weakly. "Put the sweater on. You're shivering like a little kid in a blizzard."

Realizing that he wouldn't take no for an answer, Maggie accepted the sweater gratefully, slipped it on over the black dress, and lay down on a small sofa, curling up in a fetal position for added warmth.

"Bring Donald here the minute you find him, okay?" she begged. "I need to see for myself that he's all right."

If he's all right, Sarah thought.

She hated to leave Maggie. It was very hard to walk away and leave her lying there, after everything she had been through.

But she was safe now. There were plenty of people around, and the person who had attacked her probably thought she was already dead, anyway, and wouldn't be looking for her. And he *might* be looking for Shane and Donald and Ellie.

111

Sarah and Riley hurried out into the hall.

Sarah asked, "Do you think the person who attacked her is a girl or a guy?"

"Maggie said she was dragged up that hill. She's almost as tall as me. Wouldn't it take a guy to drag her that far?"

"Maggie's tall, but she's light as a feather," Sarah argued. There were couples sitting on the stairs. She lowered her voice. The mansion was still noisy, so Riley had to strain to hear her. "Lots of girls could grab Maggie from behind, catch her off guard, and drag her. *Cass* probably could. So could some of the girls who helped her during the musical chairs game."

The people sitting on the stairs ignored Riley and Sarah. Some were studying the small yellow cards, others who had chosen not to play the game were talking and laughing. It was hard for Sarah to accept that none of the guests had a clue about what had happened to Maggie. Hadn't Cass told them anything?

Apparently not. If she had, no one seemed the least bit interested. Not enough to stop their partying.

Sarah shivered. Remembering that she and Riley had been on their way to the stables before the crash, she started heading for the front door.

"Wait a sec," Riley said suddenly, touching her elbow. "One minute, okay?"

Surprised, Sarah half turned. "What?" Her voice was impatient and tense with worry. "Riley, we have to hurry!"

"I know." He stood looking down at her. The glow of flickering light played across his face. His expression was serious, his eyes on hers. "Listen, Sarah," he said earnestly, taking both of her hands in his, "I just want to say, I wish we'd met someplace else, under different circumstances."

Sarah didn't look away. "Me, too."

"Every time you think about me now," Riley continued, "you're going to think about tonight. I hate that."

Sarah wanted fiercely to reassure Riley that tonight's horror wouldn't affect the way she felt about him. But she couldn't erase from her mind being locked in the music room, and even worse, the image of Maggie slumped over the steering wheel in that death car. One way or another, Cass Rockham was responsible. If she hadn't done it herself, someone she'd invited *had*. And Riley was Cass's friend. He was part of her crowd. Even now, after he'd seen with his own eyes what had happened to Maggie, he couldn't believe Cass was behind it. As if one of *their* crowd could never do anything so awful.

Taking a deep breath of resolve, Sarah pulled her eyes and her hands away from Riley and turned away. "Come on," she urged, "we have to hurry!"

"All right," Riley said. "But first, I want to take another look at the clues."

A group of party guests who had chosen to ignore the "people hunt" passed by. Several stopped to express interest in what Riley and Sarah were puzzling over. A husky boy named Gabe, wearing a bright red shirt, said he was sure the "loaf of bread, jug of wine" clue meant the kitchen.

Riley explained impatiently why it didn't.

A girl in a peach dress said she thought it probably meant that someone was hidden under the refreshment table in the small salon, until Sarah pointed out that they were all *in* that room when the "losers" were taken away. The girl giggled and moved away. A tall girl with blonde hair moved slightly forward in the group. "Basement pantry?" she suggested.

Sarah glanced up. "Excuse me?"

"There's a big pantry in the basement, like Cass's family is getting ready for World War III or something. Want me to show you where it is? The door locks so none of the servants can steal food, so I guess it'd make a good hiding place."

"That's probably where Maggie was hidden first," Sarah told Riley quietly. "She said she thought it was in the basement, and there were shelves with food. Maybe we should check it out. We might find a clue there."

Accompanied by Gabe and led by the girl, whose name was Gwen, they moved through the rooms to the top of the basement stairs, opened the door and began to descend.

Moaning in pain, Shane clutched her wounded hand. The black cat stared at her balefully, back still arched, ready to strike again if necessary.

"Why did you *do* that?" Shane cried, backing away awkwardly, still hunched in a crouching position. "Isn't it bad enough that I'm stuck here all alone and don't know where my friends are? Isn't it bad enough that I'm scared and I wish I'd never come? I can't believe you did that! I didn't do anything to *you*!"

It hissed contemptuously. Then it turned its back on her and retreated to its home under the table. There, it curled up in a furry ball and became a part of the darkness.

The injured hand was bleeding profusely, the ruts etched by the cat's claw pooling with red. Tears blinded her as Shane tried to search the dimly lit room with her eyes, hunting for something to wrap around her wounds.

The open French door sent in periodic gusts of wind to torment the candle flames. One came now, and the moving shadows it created illuminated a wall dotted with old portraits of men and women wearing white wigs, antique dartboards with steel-tipped darts protruding like harpoons, and a pair of framed paintings of sail-festooned ships. The settee and an old wicker rocker cushioned in a blue floral print were the only pieces of furniture besides the table holding the pair of chunky candles.

Nowhere did Shane see any sign of something that would double as a bandage.

Thick, oblong drops of blood fell to the hardwood floor. Shane stared at them with eyes glazed by pain. "You're a mean, nasty cat," she accused the black blob under the table. "Just like the mean, nasty person who locked me in here. Are you Cass's cat? Has she been giving you lessons in how to hurt and scare people?"

There was no response from beneath the table.

Shane sank back upon her heels. "This shouldn't be happening to me," she said softly. Blood from her injured hand dripped steadily onto her dress and seemed to disappear among its bright red folds. "I haven't done anything wrong. Not this time."

Chapter 16

There was no one in the basement pantry when Riley and Sarah, Gabe and Gwen arrived.

But there was, tacked directly beneath the roll of colored stickers on the wall, another ragged scrap of black paper with a chalked message.

" *What a gas, man!* " Riley read aloud. He turned to face his companion. "What a gas? What does that mean?"

Frowning, Sarah thought for a minute. "Wait a sec," she said slowly. "This is where Maggie was taken first, right? This is where Cass had her hidden? 'Shelves with food, down a flight of stairs?' This has to be it."

Riley nodded. "Right."

"Then she was taken out of here, to the garage." Sarah waved the scrap of black paper in the air. " 'What a gas, man,' is a clue. It's telling us that Maggie was taken to the garage."

While Riley immediately understood her meaning, Gabe and Gwen still looked puzzled. "A clue?" Gabe repeated.

"Sure. Whoever is moving my friends around is playing a variation of Cass's original game. Only," Sarah's voice was grim, "he's not playing. This game is deadly. And I think," she added, "that we'd better find Donald, Ellie, and Shane as soon as possible."

"Do you still have that first scrap of black paper?" Riley asked her. "The one we found outside of the upstairs closet?"

Sarah nodded. She'd thrust it into her purse for safekeeping. Taking it out, she read it again. *"Chill out, guys!"*

Riley pursed his lips. "It's telling us someone is hidden in someplace cold. A refrigerator? Freezer? Can't be. That's silly."

"No, it's not!" Gwen cried. "They have a huge walk-in freezer down here. On the other side of the basement. You could hide a person in there." She looked at Sarah, her large dark eyes very round. "But if someone's locked in there, they'd freeze to death. . . . "

"Where *is* it?" Sarah demanded. "Show us! Hurry!"

Gwen turned and briskly led them to the giant walk-in freezer, a stainless steel chamber set into the wall.

It was locked. Although Riley pulled and tugged on the handle, the door never gave an inch.

No sound came from within the huge steel box. No one was shouting for help or pounding on the metal door.

Either they were wrong and there was no captive inside, or . . .

Naked fear shrouded all four faces. They knew that the silence within the metal chamber was not a good sign.

"Where can we get a key?" Sarah asked Gwen. Anxiety pitched her voice high, thinning the words.

"Maybe the caterer?"

Without a word, Sarah turned and raced for the stairs.

But the caterer refused to give her a key. "You'll have to find Miss Rockham," the sturdy, rosy-cheeked woman told her as she pulled a tray of miniature pizzas from one of the ovens. "If she says it's okay, you can have the key. But I need to hear her say it with my own ears, Miss."

"But I'll *never* find her in this crowd!" Sarah cried in dismay. "This is an emergency, can't you understand that? Someone could be dying in that freezer!"

"Oh, I doubt that, Miss," the woman said calmly, depositing the pizzas on a warming tray. "You just find Miss Rockham and tell her all about it. Go on now, that's a good girl."

She thinks I've lost it, Sarah realized with a sinking heart. She'll probably call the men in white coats the second I leave this kitchen. And now I'm going to have to search this entire mammoth house for Cass, while one of my friends is probably freezing to death.

There wasn't time to go back downstairs and enlist Riley's or Gwen's or Gabe's aid in the search. She would have to find Cass herself. And fast!

Sarah raced from room to room, the bronze skirt

flowing out behind her, fear and anxiety etched in every line of her face.

There was no sign of Cass in the huge entry hall or in the small salon or on the stairs.

The seconds, the minutes, raced by, uncaring.

Her mind on the icy temperatures in the basement freezer, Sarah shouted Cass's name as she tore through the house, pushing people aside, ignoring their stares, bumping into tables and chairs and sofas as she ran.

"Where is Cass?" she screamed over the pounding rock music as she entered the festively decorated ballroom. She aimed her question at a group of dancers directly in front of her.

They shrugged, never missing a beat.

Sarah turned away, disheartened. She had been sure Cass would be in the ballroom, dancing the night away as if this were any ordinary party instead of the deadly disaster it had become.

Who was in that freezer, frightened, fighting the frigid temperature?

Donald? Shane? Ellie?

Sarah shoved through a pair of heavy glass doors to check out the terrace.

And found Cass, kissing a boy in a navy-blue blazer.

"Cass!" Sarah shrieked, rushing over to the startled couple. They jerked apart, annoyed. "Cass, get me the key to the basement freezer, *now!*"

Taking a step backward, Cass regarded Sarah with suspicion.

"Who *is* this?" the boy asked, staring at Sarah.

Her French braid had come loose, sending wisps of sandy hair curling around her ears. Her cheeks were flushed, her brown eyes frantic.

"You were up on the hill when that crazy redhead drove my father's Jag through the garage wall," Cass said. "How did you get out of the music room? Isn't that where Morgan put you? Why aren't you still hiding? The game isn't over yet. No one's brought me all five stickers."

Losing the last of her patience, Sarah reached out and grabbed Cass's wrist. "Oh, yes, the game *is* over!" she muttered from between clenched teeth. She began dragging her hostess toward the double glass doors. "Your stupid game is dangerous! Now, you're coming with me, and you're going to get me that key, and you'd better hope like mad that I found you in time!"

"In time for what? What are you *doing*? Let go of me!"

Sarah's head whipped around to face Cass as they reached the doors. "Listen, you viper! One of my best friends was almost killed, thanks to you, and three more are missing. They're in danger, too. One of them is probably locked in your basement freezer right now! So, unless you want someone's death on your puny little conscience, you get me that key right this minute!"

Cass got her the key.

But she refused to come downstairs with Sarah.

"I don't know what kind of stunt you and your weird friends are pulling," she said as she handed Sarah the key, "but I wish I'd never invited you."

"That makes six of us!" Sarah snapped. Then she snatched the key out of Cass's hand and ran for the basement stairs.

A minute later, she and Riley pulled open the heavy metal door and were greeted by a heavy slap of icy air.

Chapter 17

It was Donald Neeson, not Shane or Ellie, who lay on the freezer floor immediately inside the door, curled up in a little ball against the cold. He was barely conscious, his skin waxy and white, his lips bluish-purple. When they lifted him, his legs stuck out stiffly. Riley, Gabe, and Gwen carried him out and set him on the floor. Sarah quickly closed the freezer door after them.

"Is he dead?" Gwen whispered, peering over Sarah's shoulder as she knelt beside Donald.

"I'll get some blankets," Gabe offered, and hurried away.

When he'd gone, Riley knelt to check Donald's pulse. "He needs the paramedics," he said a moment later. "We have to call an ambulance."

Sarah nodded and ran upstairs.

There was a telephone on a small table in the noisy first floor hall. The area was full of people who had given up in disgust on the "people hunt." Just as Sarah reached the phone, it rang. A boy in a white T-shirt was passing by and automatically reached out to pick up the receiver.

Sarah groaned. Now the line would be tied up. And the minutes were ticking away. Where was Shane? And Ellie? Was Donald going to be all right?

"Who?" the boy shouted into the telephone. "Dane? I can't hear you! Dane who? We're having a party here. You'll have to talk louder."

Sarah hadn't intended to eavesdrop but she couldn't help overhearing.

"What? Can't hear you. Someone's after Dane? Dane who?"

Intrigued, Sarah began listening intently. With all of the weird things going on, the phrase "someone's after Dane" might be important.

Moving closer, she tugged on the boy's sleeve. "Who's on the phone?"

He shook his head. "Don't know. Some lady. She sounds like she's losing it." He replaced the receiver. "Said she wanted to talk to her kid. Dane or Zane, something like that. Said to tell the kid someone named Lynn was after her. I couldn't hear half of what she said. So I gave up."

"Someone named Lynn? Is after someone named Dane?"

"Yeah." The boy looked down at Sarah, a quizzical expression on his face. "She couldn't mean Lynn Loomis, could she?"

Sarah knew Lynn Loomis. Everyone at Greenhaven High knew him. He was running back on the varsity football team.

The boy shook his head again. "Somebody made good old Lynn mad? Heck, they better watch out.

I wouldn't want Lynn after me!" The boy walked off as Sarah grabbed the phone.

Dialing the emergency number, Sarah worked on the boy's garbled message. Dane? Zane? Could he have meant . . . Shane?

They hadn't found Shane yet. She was still missing.

Was someone after Shane? Why would Lynn Loomis be mad at Shane? He was a big guy, built like a diesel truck. He could probably lift both Maggie *and* Donald at the same time without flinching.

But if he was mad at Shane, why would he stick Maggie in that car?

It made no sense.

Except . . . she hadn't seen Lynn at the party. Shouldn't he be here? All the other football players were. So where was Lynn Loomis?

Hiding somewhere in the house? Coming out only when he was ready to kidnap another of her friends and take them to a place *he'd* chosen?

Maybe it was really *Cass* Lynn was mad at. Maybe she'd done something awful to him and now he was ruining her party as a way of getting even.

When she had completed her call, Sarah hurried back to the basement. Gwen had gone upstairs to find hot coffee for Donald. Gabe had returned to the party after supplying Donald with a pair of warm blankets. Donald was conscious, but shaking violently.

Sarah and Riley managed to get him upstairs. Riley led the way to a small den where they installed Donald on a sofa, wrapping the blankets tightly around him. He looked as if he was shrouded in a gray cocoon.

Donald's eyes widened in disbelief as Sarah told him of Maggie's narrow escape. "Are you sure she's okay?" he wanted to know when she'd finished. "Carbon monoxide poisoning is wicked stuff. How do you know she's all right?"

"She said she was. But we want her to go to the hospital with you, just so she can be checked out." Sarah forced a smile. "I'm so glad we found you when we did." Then, more intently, "Donald, who took you out of the upstairs closet? That's where you were hidden first, right? We found a piece of paper up there, with a clue on it about the freezer. But it wasn't one of Cass's clues. Who put it there? It had to be the person who took you to the freezer."

To her disappointment, Donald shook his head. "I saw zilch. *Nada.* Nothing. The door opened, someone thunked me on the head, I saw stars, and I woke up in the Antarctic. That's it. Sorry."

Gwen returned, a cup of steaming liquid in her hands. Sarah went to meet her in the doorway, taking the cup of coffee gratefully. "Could you do us a favor?" she asked. "Could you run and get Maggie? She's in a little room right near the front door. Donald wants to see her, and I guess it'll be okay if they wait here together for the ambulance. Would you mind?"

"Ah, romance," Gwen answered with a grin. "Ain't love grand? Be right back!" And she left to fetch Maggie.

Sarah took the coffee to Donald. "Maggie will be

right here," she told him as she gave him the hot cup. "You can see for yourself that she's okay."

Donald tried, and failed, to sit upright. "I don't get what's going on," he said as he carefully sipped the coffee. "What's with this party? Where's Shane? And Ellie?"

"We don't know yet." Sarah glanced at her watch. They were spending too much time with Donald, but she didn't want to leave him until Maggie arrived. "Why would anyone want to hurt Maggie? Or you?" She studied Donald's white face. There was something . . . "Donald? Do you have any ideas?"

Donald nodded reluctantly, his eyes sliding away from Sarah's. "I wish I didn't. But I think maybe it might be Dolly."

"Dolly? That girl you met at camp?"

Another nod. "I know it sounds crazy. I mean, she doesn't even live here in town, and she wouldn't know where Cass lives, but . . . " His husky voice drifted off.

"Donald," Riley pointed out, "anyone who wanted to could find out where the Rockhams live. It's the only place like it in town."

"Yeah, good point. Anyway, Dolly was really mad when I told her I was coming here without her. I mean, she sounded totally freaked out on the phone. Mad enough to do something . . . well, something crazy."

"You think this girl is strong enough to lift and carry you?" Riley asked, disbelief on his face.

Donald thought for a second. "Yeah, I think so.

She's big. She's a swimmer. She was a lifeguard at camp. She's got really strong arms and shoulders. Besides," he added, "she might not have done it all herself. Maybe she got a friend to help." He shook his head sadly. "It's really hard to believe that someone I liked would do anything so nuts. But I keep hearing the way she sounded on the phone, you know?"

"But why would she hurt Maggie?" Sarah asked, as Gwen and Maggie entered the room.

Donald, unaware of their presence, said, "Maybe Dolly figured out that Maggie was the reason I wanted to come to this party alone. I talked about you guys a lot this summer, and maybe there was something different in my voice when I mentioned Maggie. Dolly's smart. She could figure out something like that. And it would have made her really mad."

Maggie, a delighted half smile lighting her face, came around a corner of the sofa to see for herself that Donald was okay. In the shimmering candlelight, her skin looked gray to Sarah. She had a nasty, purpling lump on her forehead, dried blood on her lower lip, and her arms and hands were patchworked with bloody scratches from being pulled through the hole in the shattered windshield.

But once the initial shock of her appearance had passed, Donald didn't seem to mind that Maggie no longer looked as perfectly gorgeous as she had earlier.

She sat down on the edge of the sofa and smiled a weak smile. He didn't seem the least bit embarrassed that she had overheard his remarks about his feelings for her.

Probably made it easier for him, Sarah thought, watching them. Now he doesn't have to say it to her face. She already knows.

Gwen gestured to Sarah from the doorway. Sarah hurried to her.

"I hate to break this up," Gwen said softly, "but shouldn't we look for your other friends?"

Sarah nodded and ran back to the sofa. "We have to find Ellie and Shane," she reminded Riley. "Maggie, when the ambulance comes, you go with Donald, okay?"

"I'm not leaving here until I know Shane and Ellie are okay."

"That goes for me, too," Donald echoed. "Besides," he added, worry in his voice, "they might need an ambulance, too."

Sarah's face went white. Shane and Ellie hurt, too? "Riley, hurry!" she urged. "Donald and Maggie will be safe here. We have to find Shane and Ellie."

"Right," Riley said firmly, moving toward her. "Where do we start?"

Chapter 18

Thoroughly miserable, Ellie knew who was behind the nightmare enveloping her. It was her sister, Ruth. It had to be. Ruth had promised that Ellie would be sorry, and Ellie had never been sorrier for anything in her life than she was for opening that invitation.

She had tried to escape. It wasn't possible. The doors refused to budge, and there were no windows. None of the light switches worked, and there was no telephone.

This awful place . . . it wasn't simply that it was dark and empty and foreign. The first place had been all of those things. But it hadn't been so sickeningly hot, the way this place was. It wasn't supposed to be so awful, she knew that. It was supposed to be pleasant. But someone had done something to it to make it the most miserable place on earth. And that someone had to be Ruth.

Ellie felt sick, really sick. She had never felt so deathly ill. If she didn't get out of this place . . .

I'm going to die, she suddenly realized. This must be what dying feels like.

Why didn't her friends come and let her out of this terrible, killing place? Was Eleanor Whittier so boring, so uninteresting, so invisible, that no one even noticed when she was gone? Were her friends so busy having a good time at Cass's party that they didn't realize what Ruth Whittier had done to her baby sister?

"Ruth, how could you be so cruel?" Ellie, dizzy and sick and frightened, cried out.

But her voice rang out in the dark, unanswered.

Aware of the minutes racing by, Sarah suggested that the searchers split up. Riley agreed, although a worried frown crossed his face. Sarah saw it and felt touched by his concern. She would rather have stayed with Riley, too, but there wasn't time. They had to split up.

"I'll go straight to the stables," he suggested. "You and Gwen take the last clue."

The yellow card read, simply:

Onward and upward!

"Up?" Sarah mused aloud. "Upstairs? We already looked upstairs. There wasn't anyone there."

"I think there's an attic," Gwen said. "Did you check up there?"

Sarah shook her head. "No. I'll do it now."

"I'll go with you."

"Okay," Riley said, "you two check that out while

I see if we're right about the horse knowing the way. Meet you back here."

Before he left, he turned to Sarah and, taking her hand, drew her aside. Speaking in a low voice, he warned, "You be careful, okay? This is not a sane person we're dealing with. If he checks the music room, and you're not there, he's going to be real mad. Just watch it, please. For me?"

Then, without warning, he bent his head and kissed her, quickly but firmly. "That's for luck," he said before turning and rushing out of the house, leaving behind a stunned Sarah.

"He's cute, isn't he?" Gwen asked with a grin as Sarah returned to her side. "You're a lucky girl."

But Sarah had no time to think about Riley's kiss or what it might mean. They had to find Shane and Ellie. She could only hope and pray that it wasn't too late.

"Upstairs," Sarah urged, giving Gwen a gentle shove. "Keep your fingers crossed that Shane or Ellie or both of them will be there."

The two girls hurried up the stairs.

Shane couldn't sit on the floor, waiting, another second. She had to *do* something. It was sheer torture, sitting alone in the candle-shadowed room, with only the nasty cat under the table for company.

Why was Cass doing this to her?

Slowly climbing to her feet, gripping her throbbing, injured right hand with her left hand, Shane began pacing slowly back and forth between the settee and the wicker rocker. Maybe Cass had found out about her. Maybe after she'd mailed the invitation, someone from Rockport had told her the whole story. Cass would have been horrified by the thought of having someone in her home who had done what Shane had done.

"So," Shane murmured aloud, thinking worriedly as she spoke, "almost the minute I arrived, I was spirited off and hidden. The musical chairs game was just an excuse to get rid of me."

But . . . Eleanor had been the first to lose, not Shane. Why take Ellie away if Shane was the one you wanted to banish?

"If Cass wanted to disguise her real intention so that I wouldn't guess what was happening and cause a scene, she *would* make other people lose, too. Ellie's probably already back at the party, having a grand time, while I'm still right where Cass wants me."

Didn't anyone wonder where she had gone? Wasn't anyone looking for her? Sarah? Maggie? Didn't they miss her?

An icy hand suddenly clutched at Shane's heart, and she stopped pacing. Of course. They *all* knew! Cass had told everyone the truth, and her friends had been repelled by it.

Now, they didn't want to be her friends anymore. She couldn't blame them.

Then Shane had an even more horrible thought. What if it wasn't Cass at all? What if it were —

"No! That's not possible!" she told herself, now desperate. "Or is it?" she whispered to the flickering shadows.

Chapter 19

When Riley arrived at the stables, there were no stickers anywhere in sight. The rough wooden walls were bare. A russet mare stuck her head through the open top half of her stall door and whinnied a soft question.

"I wish you could tell me what's going on," Riley grumbled.

He was about to leave in disappointment when he noticed a door at the far end of the row of stalls. An office? Worth checking out, anyway.

And there it was, a roll of lime-green stickers on the wall beside the stable office door. He played his flashlight over the area, and when he saw another scrap of black paper fluttering in the night breeze, he realized with a stab of anger that the office was already empty. Whoever had been hidden in there had been removed.

Angry and frustrated, he ripped the scrap of paper from the wall. The chalked scrawl was so faint, he could barely read it.

But with the aid of the flashlight, he managed to decipher, *Don't sweat it, man!*

Riley concentrated. *Chill out, guys!* had meant the freezer. What would *Don't sweat it, man!* mean?

The sauna? That little redwood building Cass's mother had ordered constructed somewhere in the woods? It had only recently become operational.

But where *was* it?

A group of party guests came wandering out of the woods, laughing. They stopped nearby to study their yellow cards under the beam of a flashlight.

"Anyone know where the new sauna is?" Riley shouted.

No one did. They were much more interested in the stables, having figured out that a roll of stickers should be positioned there.

Neighing foolishly and laughing, they ambled away, toward the office.

There were several paths into the woods. Uncertain, Riley hesitated. If he chose the wrong one, he'd be wasting precious time.

A couple came into the clearing along a different path from the group's route. They were holding hands and, like the first group, laughing.

Riley envied them their carefree ignorance of the horrible events of the evening. They were simply having a good time.

Why hadn't this terror touched anyone but Sarah and her friends? What was it about them that had someone angry enough to kill? And what part in this nightmare had Cass played by inviting them?

Did she know more than she was telling?

"The sauna back that way?" he asked, hope in his voice.

"Nope," the boy answered. "Nothin' but woods and owls back there. Maybe a few bats."

The girl squealed in fake terror. Laughing, they walked away.

That left only one possible path.

Aiming his flashlight in front of him, he ran.

Ellie was having difficulty breathing. Her body was soaking wet, and the pale green fabric of her dress stuck to her like another layer of skin.

Her chest hurt. Each time it moved in and out in an effort to breathe, pain squeezed it, as if someone had encircled it with a huge vise. Her head felt swollen to twice its normal size.

Why doesn't someone come to get me? she wondered, before she gave up and closed her eyes.

Shane was pacing again. The party was still in full swing. She could hear distant laughter and music, and she pictured Maggie and Donald, Sarah and Ellie all dancing and laughing and having a grand time. Even if Cass had told them the truth about her, shouldn't they have given her a chance to explain? It didn't seem like them to take the word of someone like Cass without checking out the story first.

Not that the story could have been denied. The truth was bad enough. But . . . some people had different ways of seeing the truth.

"I made a mistake," she murmured aloud. "I was stupid. And I've been sorry ever since. A lot of good *that* does!"

Shane was snapped out of her misery by the sound of sudden footsteps just outside the door.

A key turned slowly in the lock and the knob moved, slowly, slowly, as if deliberately torturing her. And then the door opened.

Shane gasped and took a step backward. Her hands began shaking as they flew to her face.

"No," she whispered, "no. It can't be."

Chapter 20

The little redwood building sat in a clearing deep in the woods. It was completely dark and looked empty. But Riley knew it was the right place when he saw the thick slab of wood slipped through the big copper door handles, barring any exit from the building. Whoever was in there was unquestionably trapped.

Running to the double doors, Riley yanked the board from between the handles and pulled one of the doors open.

And walked into an inferno of steam heat.

A girl in a pale green dress lay sprawled across the wooden floor like some ailing sea creature. Sodden hair clung limply to her pale cheeks, shiny with perspiration. Her eyes were rolled back in her head, and her chest moved with effort, but she was breathing. Barely.

He remembered her. She'd been the first person to lose at musical chairs, and had given Sarah a helpless, confused look, like a trapped animal.

Riley glanced at the round control gauge on the

wall beside the door. The black arrow was deep inside the red section where the letters DANGER were printed.

He didn't need to check the gauge to know that someone had tampered with it deliberately, making it impossible for the girl to adjust the temperature and save herself.

The first thing he needed to do was get the poor girl out of this oven. He was having trouble breathing himself. Staggering under Ellie's damp, leaden weight, Riley struggled to the door and outside, where he carefully put her down on the cool, dewy grass. Then he took a deep breath and raced up the path. The girl in the green dress needed medical help, and she needed it fast.

Had he found her in time?

As Shane took another involuntary step backward, the backs of her knees struck the settee, knocking her off balance. She fell into a sitting position, her hands covering her mouth, her eyes wide with horror.

Like a vision straight out of one of Shane's frequent nightmares, Lynn was standing in front of her, grinning.

Shane had tried hard to dismiss the idea that Lynn might somehow be behind all this. Now, with the person she feared most entering the room, Shane realized her suspicions had been right all along.

She would never forget the rage, the anger, the hatred in Lynn's voice that last time. "You're going to leave me here to face the music alone?" had been Lynn's furious reaction to the news that Shane's parents were selling their home at the very height of the scandal and moving away. "Now, when everyone in town is talking about us, pointing at us, whispering behind our backs? You're going to take off and leave me to face this *alone*? You can't do that, Shane. You can't! We were supposed to be in this together."

And when Shane had explained timidly that she had no choice, that the decision belonged to her parents and they thought leaving was the right thing to do for the whole family, Lynn had attacked her physically, shouting hateful, ugly things, and threatening real harm.

Shane's father, hearing the shouting, had run in from the den and intervened, narrowly saving Shane from a broken jaw . . . or worse.

But her father wasn't here to rescue her now.

"What are you doing here?" Shane repeated as her visitor approached. "How did you get in here?"

Lynn took a seat in the wicker chair opposite Shane. The flickering candlelight bathed the room in an eerie yellowish glow.

Like the inside of a jack-o'-lantern, Shane thought, and shook with dread.

Before Lynn could answer Shane's questions, they were interrupted by the wail of an ambulance siren. Its nervous wail overwhelmed the fainter party sounds, and sent Shane's mind spinning back to another night, months ago, when the shrieking had come not from an ambulance, but from a police car. . . .

Riley flagged down the ambulance as it screeched to a halt in front of the mansion's wide stone steps. The girl in the green dress needed help more desperately than Donald and Maggie. He led the two paramedics, stretcher in tow, into the woods to the sauna.

"She's in a bad way," one of the paramedics told him when they reached the stricken girl lying motionless on the ground in front of the little cedar building. "She's lucky we got here in time."

"There are two more up at the house," Riley said wearily. "I'll go tell them you're here."

Maggie and Donald were relieved to hear that Ellie had been found. Riley was careful to avoid the details of her condition, not wanting to alarm them.

"Gwen and Sarah haven't come back downstairs yet," Maggie told Riley. "So I'm afraid they haven't found Shane."

Riley didn't like the sound of that. He'd been gone quite a while. Why hadn't Sarah come back?

No point in worrying Maggie and Donald. Neither of them looked too great. Donald's face was still bone-white, and Maggie's an unhealthy gray. The lump on her forehead had turned an ugly purplish-red and stuck out like a doorknob.

"You guys go on now," he said with a calmness he didn't feel. "The paramedics say Ellie can't wait. They'll take the three of you to the hospital."

Maggie hesitated. She hated to leave without making sure Shane was okay.

Seeing her reluctance to leave, Donald took Maggie's hand in his. "Come with me?" he said quietly.

Keeping her hand in Donald's, Maggie asked Riley, "But you'll bring Sarah and Shane to the hospital the minute you find them, right?"

He nodded and helped her and Donald out into the hall and down the steps to the waiting ambulance.

"I mean it, Riley," Maggie insisted as she climbed into the back of the emergency vehicle. "I want to see for myself that they're okay."

When the rear doors closed, Riley was left with the dismal picture of Ellie lying unconscious on one cot, Donald on another, and a forlorn Maggie, worried about her friends, sitting beside Donald's cot, unwilling to release her hold on his hand.

Riley shook his head as he turned away and hurried back into the house. What a sorry sight! Three sick, injured people who had no idea why this night had become, for them, a disaster.

Behind him, the ambulance shrieked away, its siren quickly fading.

Now . . . he had to find Sarah.

He quickened his steps.

When Riley reached the porch, he found Cass waiting for him. There was no alarm or concern in her face, only annoyance.

"That's what I get for inviting outsiders," she said with disgust, gesturing down the hill in the direction the ambulance had taken. "They've absolutely ruined my party!"

Riley stared at her, his dark eyes cold with contempt. "You're blaming *them*? Cass, three people almost died! And one is still missing. This is all your doing. You and your stupid games."

He turned to stomp away, but Cass followed.

"Riley," she said tersely, "I don't see how you can blame me for everything that's happened. If you ask me, your new friends brought their trouble with them. Nothing like this has ever happened at my parties before. Doesn't it look like it's all *their* doing?"

"Maybe you planned it that way." Riley frowned. "I just can't figure out why. You're spoiled and selfish, Cass, but I never thought of you as crazy. Maybe I just wasn't paying attention."

He turned away from her then. "Now, leave me alone," he called over his shoulder as he hurried to the phone in the entry hall. "I have to call the police."

And before she could protest, he'd dialed the number.

Chapter 21

As Shane sat, looking at Lynn, her mind was far away, recalling that night, months ago.

The policemen hadn't done the things she'd feared. No handcuffs. No reading of rights. She was a juvenile, as was Lynn, and they hadn't been mistreated. She'd been too frightened to tell them her name. They'd had to look in her purse for identification.

And then they'd called her parents.

Lynn hadn't spoken at all, either. But that silence had come from defiance, not fear.

Even now, after she'd gone over it in her head hundreds of times, Shane still wasn't quite sure how Lynn had talked her into it. But Lynn was always good at getting what she wanted, at convincing people. She was very . . . persuasive, when she wanted to be. And she had persuaded Shane.

Shane's thoughts were abruptly brought back to the present time.

"Didn't I tell you I could find you anywhere?" Lynn asked. "You didn't believe me, Shane. That was stupid of you. I never lie about stuff like that."

"No, but you *do* lie," Shane murmured, anger beginning to rise within her. This shouldn't be happening to her. The whole, ugly mess of months ago was supposed to be behind her. Over and done with. The judge had put them both on probation and released them to their parents. He had later given her parents permission to move to Greenhaven because it was in the same county. He had sternly urged her to "take advantage of this new opportunity and get your life together."

And wasn't that what she'd been trying to do?

But how could she when the past was sitting, an evil grin on its face, right there in front of her?

"You lied about the ring," Shane continued bravely. "You said it was just cheap costume jewelry. And it wasn't. Five thousand dollars isn't cheap costume jewelry, Lynn. We could have gone to jail for a long time. And you lied about *me*. You told everyone it was *my* idea. It wasn't. It was yours."

Her visitor said nothing, but continued to regard Shane with that sly, wicked grin.

"Was that stupid musical chairs game downstairs your idea?" Shane demanded. "Did you talk Cass into helping you do this? I know better than anyone how good you are at talking people into doing things for you."

The thin, mean slit of a mouth opened then. "Don't be stupid! I don't even know the rich girl who owns this house. And I don't want to. Who needs her? I did this all by myself. That's the way

I prefer it now." The voice lowered. "Who needs people? They just turn on you, anyway, especially when you're in trouble. Look how the whole town turned on us."

"It was our own fault, Lynn. We never should have . . ." Shane swallowed past the lump in her throat. It was so hard to say the words out loud. "We never should have tried to steal that ring."

Saying the words, giving the terrible memory a voice, brought it all flooding back in a bleak wash of shame. It played itself across her mind as if she were watching it on one of Cass's television screens.

She didn't want to watch. She wouldn't. Not again!

But she was powerless to erase the images once they began. Unable to stop herself, she relived again every miserable, frightening moment of it.

It had been a Thursday night. The mall was crowded, but Lynn said that was an advantage, that it would be easier to slip out of the jewelry store unnoticed.

They had planned carefully. Lynn knew exactly when the security guard would take his break. No one replaced him during his absence. Shane's job was to distract the lone salesclerk while her companion pocketed the ring from a tray on display. Lynn had seen it done in the movies dozens of times, and it had always seemed to work.

But that was the movies. Not real life.

And it had seemed to be working . . . at first. Shane dropped her purse and sent lipstick and coins and breath mints and tiny pieces of notepaper and snapshots and tissues and pencils and pens splashing out across the expensive gray carpet. The salesclerk exclaimed in dismay over the mess and hurried over to help Shane retrieve her belongings and stuff them back into her black shoulderbag.

While Lynn pocketed the ring.

That part of it went smoothly.

But as the pair walked out the door, being very careful not to hurry or look the least bit guilty or furtive, an alarm sounded throughout the mall. The noise sounded to Shane like a million clanging fire engines, a million ringing bells, a million cymbals meeting. It froze her feet to the floor and stopped her pulse.

Still, for a moment she was able to pretend that the screaming sound had nothing to do with her own actions. Denial kept her from passing out or breaking into a frantic race down the corridor, away from the store.

But when the salesclerk came rushing over, his face as white as Lynn's T-shirt, and grabbed each of them by an elbow and dragged them back inside the store, reality kicked her solidly in the stomach, punching the breath out of her.

During the only second when they were alone after that, in a moment when the manager and the salesclerk were conferring in private outside of the locked office where Shane and Lynn waited, Lynn had shrugged and said, "The price tag must have had a code in it that set off the alarm. I guess I should have checked that part out. If I'd known, I

147

could have dumped the price tag right there on the counter. Well, live and learn, right?"

Lynn's hastily concocted story about having taken the ring "by mistake," a simple error that "anyone could have made," failed to impress the clerk or the manager and, later, the police. The manager, a heavy-set balding man in a gray suit, silenced Lynn's excuses with one cold, unforgiving look. His expression remained stony and unrelenting as the three of them waited in silence for the mall security guard.

He didn't buy the story, either, and immediately called the town police.

They arrived minutes later. Then the nightmare really began.

Curious shoppers, seeing the police arrive, came into the store to stare. Seeing the pair in the office, surrounded by uniformed law officers, they began whispering behind their hands, shaking their heads.

Then came the humiliation of being marched through the store, past the onlookers, and then down miles and miles and miles of mall corridor to the front entrance.

Passing people from school who knew her, seeing them gasp in disbelief.

Passing friends of her parents, out shopping for spring clothes for their kids, staring and clucking their tongues.

Passing a boy she liked, watching his face flush with embarrassment . . . for her.

Until that moment, she had never wanted to die, had never even thought about it. True, she wasn't the most popular girl in school. She was too shy, too uncertain about herself. But she had Lynn, who was more forceful, more outgoing, and they had fun together.

So she had never wanted her life to end.

Until that night at the mall.

But the tile floor, clicking under her boot heels, adamantly refused to open and swallow her up, although she prayed fiercely for it to do just that.

Shane had thought nothing could be worse than that long, tortuous walk of shame.

But she'd been wrong.

The worst moment came when Lynn began to lie.

"It was Shane's idea. She wanted that ring more than anything. She told me if I didn't get it for her, she'd make my life miserable."

And the more the lies were stubbornly repeated, the more Shane realized that the person telling them was beginning to believe it was true. Lynn now believed every word coming from the same mouth that had told Shane, "We won't get caught, honest! I could do this in my sleep, it's so easy. Quit being such a chicken!"

Lynn was now blaming her. When the actual truth was exactly the opposite. Not that it mattered whose idea it was. They were both guilty.

But because the ring had been recovered and because of their ages, they hadn't gone to jail.

Their punishment had been of a different kind. In a small town, word travels fast. And it wasn't the kind of small town that had much tolerance for criminals, no matter what their age.

*The aftermath had been brutal. Until Shane's
parents gave up and decided the only solution was
to leave Rockport for good.*

*Lynn hadn't been so lucky. Mr. and Mrs. Block
couldn't afford to move, even if they'd wanted to.*

*They didn't. They felt a lesson was better learned
if the wrongdoer "faced the consequences."*

"My parents never forgave me," Lynn said now,
interrupting Shane's miserable memories. "I had to
move out of the house. Out of my own home. No
one in town would talk to me, except the creeps.
People looked the other way when I walked down
the street. No one called and no one answered *my*
calls. It was like having some horrible, contagious
disease."

"I'm sorry," Shane said softly.

"Shut up! After you left, after you ran away with
your parents, leaving me there all alone, I had nobody. I was completely, totally alone." The voice
grew harsher, cold as ice. "The whole thing was
your doing. You talked me into stealing that ring.
And then you deserted me. I can never forgive you
for that, Shane."

"No . . . it wasn't like that, and you know it.
Why have you forgotten the way it really was?"

"Liar, liar, liar! If your precious new friends
knew what a liar you are, they'd never have spoken
to you. They shouldn't have." Lynn's expression
grew dark and grim, eyebrows meeting in an angry
scowl. "They should have known better than to
make friends with someone like you. You'd just be-

tray them, the way you betrayed me."

Shane sat up straighter. "My friends? What do you know about my friends?" Her stomach became knotted with fresh fear. Was that why they hadn't come for her? Had Lynn done something to them?

"Lynn," she said evenly, leaning forward, "what have you done to my friends?"

Chapter 22

Shane knew she had to stall for time. The distant laughter and music had been replaced by the sound of countless car engines starting and then departing. The party was over. Now someone would realize she was missing and come looking for her.

"What I did to your stupid new friends," Lynn said coldly in answer to Shane's question, "I'm going to do to you. They're dead. I killed them. All but one. She got away. But I'll take care of her later, when I've finished with you."

Shane stopped breathing. No! Lynn was lying. It wasn't possible. No one could kill four people at a party crowded with guests. That was crazy. Someone would have stopped something so horrible from happening. The idea was, simply, insane. . . .

Then Shane remembered the wail of the ambulance and looked into Lynn's eyes. Insane? Shane felt sick. Was that what she saw in those eyes? Insanity? Was that what had happened to Lynn when their world fell apart around the two of them?

If my friends are dead, she thought despairingly,

it's because of me. I should never have tried to have friends again.

Scooting backward on the settee until she felt the wall pressing into her spine, she forced herself to calm her screaming nerves and still her pounding heart. After a moment, she was able to ask in a conversational tone of voice, "How did you find out about this party? How did you know I'd be here? Or who my friends were?" Oh, God, make it be a lie, she prayed. Don't let my friends be hurt or dead, please! "I'm not a friend of the girl who lives in this house. She only invited us to play a trick on us."

"I know." Lynn's need to explain the cleverness of her plan to punish Shane overcame her, and she began talking. "I've been in town two weeks. I heard about this bash and figured you'd be going. I mean," the face twisted with contempt, "considering how you're building a new life and all. I've been watching you. I know all about your new friends." A sneer twisted the lips. "I think they're all jerks, frankly. Don't know what you see in any of them."

Lynn hadn't said "what you *saw* in them." No past tense, there. So maybe it was a lie, Shane thought. Maybe her friends were okay. They *had* to be.

But then, why the ambulance?

"I slipped in with the caterer's staff this afternoon when they were being given a tour of the house and grounds. No one even noticed me. That's how I know my way around so well. I also stole a batch of the yellow cards your hostess planned to pass out at the party. It took me about two minutes to figure out where everyone was hidden."

Shane watched in shocked fascination as Lynn boasted about such clever tactics. Lynn had gained weight since last spring. Her face was puffy, with a slight yellowish tinge to it. Her eyes were fever-bright, her hair a lifeless clump of muddy brown. It needed cutting.

If I'd run into Lynn on the street, Shane thought sadly, I'm not sure I would have known who she was. The scandal had taken a terrible toll.

But she couldn't afford to feel sorry for the wild-eyed creature in front of her. Sympathy would only lower her defenses against this person who intended to harm her. And that mistake might cost her her life.

I don't want my life to end, she thought clearly. This has been my worst year, and there've been so many times when I didn't want to get out of bed and face the world again. But I did it.

After a while, Shane had realized that no matter how horrible her life was, Monday still became Tuesday and Tuesday became Wednesday and Wednesday became Thursday. . . . The world didn't stop just because she wished that it would.

And it had even begun to seem possible, just possible, that when enough Mondays and Tuesdays and Wednesdays had passed, the memory of that horrible night in the mall would fade, just a little.

That hope, feeble as it was, had made it easier to keep going, to pack up and go with her parents to Greenhaven, to live in a new house and make new friends.

She was making a new life.

A life that Lynn had every intention of taking from her.

While Riley phoned the police, Cass sent everyone home. Indignant groans greeted her announcement that the party was over. But when she added that the police were on their way due to "an unfortunate accident," the mansion cleared quickly. No one wanted to be included in any trouble.

"This is the worst night of my life!" Cass exclaimed in exasperation as Riley hung up the phone. Her lower lip thrust forward. "I thought the musical chairs game and the people hunt would be fun. Scavenging for people instead of things is such a neat idea. It should have been a great party."

"Oh, sure," Riley said, his voice stern, "scavenging for people is just great, as long as it isn't people you give a hoot about. You invited five people to this house to *use* them, Cass, for entertainment. And now those five people are in serious trouble. Three of them have been hurt already. And we don't know where the other one is. And now, I don't even know where Sarah is. Where did you hide Sarah's friend, Cass? Shane Magruder? Maybe we'll get lucky and she'll still be there. And I just hope Sarah is with her."

Cass looked blank. "Shane? I don't know which one she is. So how can I know where she's hiding?"

"The clue said 'Onward and Upward!' " Riley said impatiently. "Does that mean anything?"

Cass's face cleared. "Oh, that's the attic. The third floor. She must be up there." She waited expectantly, a half smile on her lips as if she expected Riley to congratulate her for her cleverness.

Instead, he turned and bolted for the stairs.

Not knowing what else to do, Cass followed.

They had reached the second floor and were about to continue on up the stairs when a tall, slender figure in a bronze-colored dress staggered out of a room, one hand to her head. Her fingers were splattered with bright red, her face pale gray. She clutched at the wall for support, leaving a scarlet handprint on the smooth white surface.

With a sharp intake of breath, Riley rushed to her side. Clutching her around the waist as her knees gave, he cried, "Sarah! My God, what happened?"

Sarah's brown eyes were glazed with shock. "I . . . I don't know. Gwen and I were almost to the attic stairs when something slammed into my head. The next thing I knew, I was lying on the floor in the bedroom." Then she looked up at Riley, worry written across her face. "Did you find Shane?"

He shook his head. "Not yet. We were on our way to the attic when you came out of that room. Cass, go call an ambulance. Now!"

"No!" Sarah protested. "I don't need one. I just have a rotten headache, that's all. I'm fine. We'd better look for Gwen. She could be hurt worse than me."

"Who's Gwen?" Cass asked irritably. "I thought we were looking for someone named Shane. Is Gwen another one of this girl's friends?"

Riley gave her a disgusted look. "No, she's one of *yours*. Don't you even remember your guests' names, Cass? Your friend Gwen has been helping us look for Sarah's friends because she knows the house and grounds better than I do."

"Gwen?" Cass frowned. "Riley, I don't know anyone named Gwen."

"That's enough talking," Lynn told Shane, who was huddled in a little ball on the settee. "You're stalling for time. You think you're so clever. But I'm the one who planned all of this, and it worked, so that makes me smarter than you, doesn't it?"

Shane couldn't keep her eyes off the open French door. If she opened her mouth and screamed, would someone hear her and rush to help her? Now that the party was over, was there anyone left on the grounds or in the house? Had Cass gone somewhere for an after-party celebration?

The sickening realization that if Lynn had been lying about what she'd done to Shane's friends, one of them would have come looking for her by now, made her ill. Because no one *had*.

Lynn reached behind her and pulled something forward. It gleamed in the candlelight. It was long and part of it was wide and . . . silvery. A knife. Lynn was holding in her right hand a wicked-looking butcher knife, and the glint in her eyes as she smiled at Shane said that she had every intention of using it. On Shane.

Shane opened her mouth to scream. But no sound escaped.

Smiling, smiling, Lynn sliced the air with the knife once, twice . . . and then she got up from the rocker and began moving toward Shane.

Chapter 23

When Sarah, Riley, and Cass burst through the door to the attic, shouting Shane's name, they came to an abrupt halt.

Shane, half-fainting with fear, was standing in the center of the room. She was in one piece, conscious and appeared unbloodied. But she was not alone.

A big girl with matted brown hair, wearing the same clothes they'd seen on the girl they knew as Gwen, was standing directly behind Shane, her chin level with the top of Shane's head. Her left arm was fastened firmly around Shane's neck, with the other arm poised above Shane's head, grasping a large knife.

"That isn't Gwen, is it?" Sarah whispered to Riley. "Gwen has blonde hair. But she's wearing Gwen's clothes."

The knife-wielder laughed harshly. "Haven't you ever heard of wigs, you stupid twit? I couldn't take a chance on Shane spotting me before I did my thing. And this isn't exactly party hair you're looking at." The voice became bitter. "I haven't exactly been motivated lately to fix myself up. Shane can understand that, can't you, Shane?"

Riley took a step forward.

"Come one step closer," Shane's captor threatened, "and this knife slits her throat. I don't mind having an audience, but you will *not* interfere!" The voice lowered, became firm with purpose. "Because I have to finish this."

She obviously meant what she said. Instead of advancing further into the room, Riley, Sarah, and Cass moved sideways, their backs close to the wall, until they were directly opposite Shane and her tormentor.

"But . . ." Sarah stammered, "you helped us! You told us where Donald was and you mentioned the attic."

The girl they'd known as Gwen laughed again. "Oh, that was so much fun! It was hilarious. The most fun I've had in ages. Thanks." She shrugged. "I wanted some entertainment while I was waiting to take care of Shane. I knew Cass would send everyone away when the police were called. I didn't mind waiting until the house was empty. Not when I was having so much fun."

"Sarah," Shane whispered, "you're alive! She said . . . Are Donald and Maggie and Ellie okay?" Her face was completely drained of all color, her blue eyes huge with fear.

Sarah nodded.

Shane sagged with relief.

"I know you," Lynn said to Sarah. "You're the one who escaped from the music room. I suppose you think you're pretty clever."

"Shane," Riley said carefully in a quiet, even voice, "what's going on? You know Gwen?"

"Gwen?" Shane's voice was barely a whisper. "This is Lynn. I knew her in Rockport. We were . . . we were friends."

Lynn? Sarah remembered the warning telephone call. Not Lynn Loomis, the football player. *This* was Lynn. Someone — maybe Mrs. Magruder — must have seen Lynn in town and guessed that she was looking for Shane. She must have called to warn Shane.

"We were *best* friends!" Lynn cried angrily, tightening her grip around Shane's neck. "I was Shane's only true friend. Since sixth grade. We shared everything." Her upper lip curled nastily. "At least, I thought we did. But I was wrong. We didn't share trouble, did we, Shane? You let me have that all for myself." Another rough wrench of Shane's neck. "*So* generous of you!"

"Shane, what is she talking about?" Sarah asked, her face very pale. "What is going on? Why is she doing this?"

Before Shane could answer, Lynn shouted, "You think your pretty little friend here is so sweet, so proper. Well, she's not! She's a common thief, that's what she is!"

Shane's eyes closed in pain.

Sarah gasped.

Cass looked nervous. A thief? In her house?

"Yes, a thief. I see you're shocked. You should be." Lynn bent her head to peer down into Shane's upturned face. "You see, Shane? Your new friends are respectable people. They won't have anything more to do with you now. So it did you no good to run away, none at all." Another grin, a mirthless baring of teeth. "If you were going to live, you'd suffer now as I have. No friends. No fun. No life. Treated like a leper, the way I was. You'd see what I've suffered, how horrible it's been."

"Then let me live," Shane gasped through Lynn's iron grip. "Punish me that, way, Lynn. If you kill me, I'll never know what you went through, will I?"

A sound of disgust followed the plea. "Oh, you're clever, Shane!" Lynn lifted her head to fix dark eyes on the scarcely breathing onlookers. "Isn't she clever? Trying to trick me into letting her live her worthless life. Just like she tricked me into stealing that ring."

"No . . . no, I didn't, Lynn! You've got it all twisted. That's not what happened." Her eyes on Sarah, Shane added, "I helped Lynn steal a ring from a jewelry store. We got caught." Shame coated her words. "I did it because I didn't want to lose my friend. But then we moved, and I lost her, anyway. Now she hates me." Her voice fell to a whisper. "I'm sorry, Sarah. Sorry for all of this."

"Shut *up!*" Lynn grabbed a fistful of Shane's hair and yanked her head back and forth as if she were a rag doll, using the same hand that held the knife.

Unable to watch the movements of the knife so close to Shane's head, Sarah looked down. And saw, with renewed shock, Shane's bloody right hand. Had Lynn done that?

"If it's Shane you want," Cass remarked petulantly, "why pick on anyone else? You almost killed one of my guests in the garage earlier. Not to mention the two in the freezer and sauna. Why'd you pick on them?"

"Because they made friends with her," Lynn answered calmly. "They shouldn't have done that. Shane doesn't deserve friends. She betrays them. So she can't have any. The others should have known that and ignored her. But they didn't. So they were punished. Enough talking!" Lynn began dragging Shane backward toward the open French door.

Sarah could see beyond it to a small iron balcony . . . three stories above the ground.

"I'm not going to kill her," Lynn said softly, a sly smile on her face. "I don't have to. All I have to do is get her out onto that balcony. I know everything there is to know about Shane. I know that heights make her dizzy and sick. She'll topple right over, and I won't have to lift a finger. I can just stand there and watch when she hits the ground and breaks into a million pieces."

"There's a safety railing on that balcony," Cass said smugly. "She won't fall."

Lynn laughed. "There's no safety rail there now.

A few turns of a screwdriver, no big deal. That balcony is as wide open as your mouth is, Cass. She'll fall, I promise you. Want to watch?"

The three watched silently as Shane's eyes pleaded for help while Lynn dragged her closer, closer to the blackness beyond the door.

Chapter 24

"I'm not going out there," Shane whispered even as Lynn continued to drag her backward. Shane's high heels dug into the hardwood floor in a futile effort to halt her progress across the room. A devilish breeze from outside set the candle flames dancing across the pair, shrouding them in eerie black and yellow shadows. "I'm not! I can't! Please, Lynn . . ." Shane's eyes, full of entreaty, turned to Sarah's face.

"Sarah, help me," she moaned. "Don't let Lynn take me out there!"

Sarah felt her own eyes fill with helpless tears. She had never seen anyone so terrified.

Lynn is right, Sarah thought with sickening conviction. Shane is so scared, she'll fall off that balcony to her death the second that Lynn gets her out there. None of us could reach her soon enough to stop her from falling.

Riley stood in front of Sarah, in hopes of making a move toward Lynn at the first opportunity.

Sarah began surreptitiously edging backward.

Because she was already only inches from the wall, her movements were almost imperceptible in the shadowy room.

The faint wail of a siren sounded in the distance.

But Sarah knew there wasn't time to wait for the police. Lynn had heard the wail, too. She tightened her grip on a struggling Shane's neck and began dragging in earnest.

As they reached the last inch of solid wooden attic floor, Shane's face crumpled and her knees caved in.

"You'll go to prison," Riley said quietly, his face as colorless as Shane's. His body was stiff with tension as he fought the need to act, conscious of the knife poised above Shane's throat. "If Shane dies, you'll spend the rest of your life there."

Sarah's back bumped up against the antique dartboard she'd spotted earlier. One of the steel-tipped darts imbedded in its surface poked her between the shoulder blades.

Keep talking, Riley, she ordered mentally, keep Lynn busy so she doesn't notice me.

Lynn laughed in response to Riley's remark. "Prison? Do you think I care about prison? My life is ruined, anyway. No friends, no family . . . no one trusts me or wants me around. Maybe in prison I'd have friends again. And if I don't, so what? At least, Shane won't be having the time of her life here with you people."

Sarah's right arm slipped behind her and began inching upward.

Lynn took another step backward, the knife still upraised, until she was standing on the balcony, her face in almost-total darkness.

Shane was only half-conscious, her eyelids flickering in terror.

Sarah's arm moved up, up, up . . . her fingers closed around her target. She clutched the needle-pointed dart, tugged on it, yanked at it awkwardly, and pulled it from the board.

"Riley," she whispered shakily in his ear, "get ready!"

He had enough presence of mind to make no sign that he'd heard. But she noticed with satisfaction that his body leaned forward slightly.

Sarah's heart was threatening to burst out of her chest, her knees felt like water, and the worst thing was, her hands were damp with clammy sweat, including the hand gripping the dart. Its cold, sharp point pressed into her wrist.

I will only have *one* chance, Sarah thought as she slowly, slowly, brought her right arm around in front of her, keeping it low, shielded by Riley. If I miss . . .

I can't miss. I can't!

Her hand was shaking violently. She had to stop that. Using every ounce of concentration, she willed it to stop. To steady itself.

Sirens shrieked to a halt nearby.

But there was no more time. Lynn was dragging Shane out onto the balcony, the knife still raised at Shane's throat.

At the very second that Lynn yanked the sagging Shane out onto the balcony, Sarah lifted her arm, took aim, and threw the dart.

At the same time, she screamed at Riley to grab Shane.

The metal tip of the dart flew through the air like a missile and slammed into the center of Lynn's right wrist, still gripping the knife.

A high, shrill shriek of pain came from Lynn's open mouth, and the knife fell to the floor of the stone balcony with a sharp smacking sound.

Riley dove, grabbing Shane's arm, yanking her to safety inside the room. The two fell in a heap on the wooden floor.

Lynn clutched at her wrist, the dart imbedded deeply in the skin. A bewildered expression crossed her face. Her lips parted as if she were about to ask a question, and her eyes were confused as she struggled to maintain her balance on the tiny stone balcony. Her arms waved wildly, clutching at the air for support.

But there was nothing . . . just as there would have been nothing for Shane to grasp onto.

With a sad, surprised look on her face, Lynn took an involuntary half-step backward that sent her over the edge of the balcony.

She never screamed. There was not a sound as she plummeted downward.

When Sarah could move again, she rushed to help Riley and Shane.

Cass moved forward to lean out cautiously, gripping the edge of the open door. The yellow floodlights along the terrace roof far below cast a dull glow over the lawn. She could barely make out the figure of a still, lifeless form surrounded by uniformed men. "They all look like the miniature metal people in my father's electric train set," she murmured.

Then, "I think she's dead," she said unnecessarily. "And the police are here. God, I may never give another party again!"

Shane began sobbing uncontrollably. Riley put his arms around her and held her gently, letting her cry.

After a few minutes, Shane took a breath and looked up at Sarah, kneeling by her side.

"You saved my life," she whispered. "I thought you'd hate me. But you saved me."

Sarah shook her head and found that she had just enough energy left to give Shane a small grin.

Shane, white-faced, tear-streaked, smiled an exhausted but beautiful smile of relief.

Riley reached out and took Sarah's hand.

About the Author

DIANE HOH grew up in Warren, Pennsylvania, "a lovely small town on the Allegheny River." Since then, she has lived in New York State, Colorado, and North Carolina. She and her family finally settled in Austin, Texas, where they plan to stay. "Reading and writing take up most of my life," says Ms Hoh, "along with family, music, and gardening."

GREEN WATCH by Anthony Masters

BATTLE FOR THE BADGERS
Tim's been sent to stay with his weird Uncle Seb and his
two kids, Flower and Brian, who run Green Watch – an
environmental pressure group. At first Tim thinks they're
a bunch of cranks – but soon he finds himself battling to
save badgers from extermination . . .

SAD SONG OF THE WHALE
Tim leaps at the chance to join Green Watch on an anti-
whaling expedition. But soon, he and the other members of
Green Watch, find themselves shipwrecked and fighting
for their lives . . .

DOLPHIN'S REVENGE
The members of Green Watch are convinced that Sam
Jefferson is mistreating his dolphins – but how can they
prove it? Not only that, but they must save Lonér, a wild
dolphin, from captivity . . .

MONSTERS ON THE BEACH
The Green Watch team is called to investigate a suspected
radiation leak. Teddy McCormack claims to have seen
mutated crabs and sea-plants, but there's no proof, and
Green Watch don't know whether he's crazy or there's
been a cover-up . . .

GORILLA MOUNTAIN
Tim, Brian and Flower fly to Africa to meet the Bests, who
are protecting gorillas from poachers. But they are
ambushed and Alison Best is kidnapped. It is up to them to
rescue her *and* save the gorillas . . .

SPIRIT OF THE CONDOR
Green Watch has gone to California on a surfing holiday –
but not for long! Someone is trying to kill the Californian
Condor, the bird cherished by an Indian tribe – the Daiku
– without which the tribe will die. Green Watch must
struggle to save both the Condor and the Daiku . . .